**"I'LL MAKE MY OWN DEAL,"
STARBUCK SAID, "BUT I NEED
SOMEONE TO OPEN THE DOOR. . . .**

"Way I hear it, them Chinamen won't traffic with just anybody when it comes to slave girls," Luke went on, eyeing O'Brien, the Barbary Coast crime czar.

"You plan to buy them outright, then?"

"For a fact," Starbuck said with cheery vigor. "An even hundred."

"A hundred?" O'Brien repeated, suddenly dumbstruck. "You mean to buy a *hundred* slave girls?"

"I like round numbers. 'Course, I'm not after just any girls." Starbuck paused, admired the tip of his cigar. "They've got to be virgins."

"Virgins!" O'Brien stared at him with a burlesque leer of disbelief. "You want a hundred *virgins?*"

Starbuck let the idea percolate for a few moments. "All virgins and the whole kit and caboodle ages twelve to sixteen . . ."

Other books by Matt Braun

THE SPOILERS
Matt Braun

PINNACLE BOOKS NEW YORK

THE SPOILERS

Copyright © 1981 by Matt Braun

A Pinnacle Books edition, published by special arrangement with the author.

Pocket Books edition/April 1981
Pinnacle edition/August 1985

ISBN: 0-523-42458-2
Can. ISBN: 0-523-43549-5

Printed in the United States of America

PINNACLE BOOKS, INC.
1430 Broadway
New York, New York 10018

9 8 7 6 5 4 3 2 1

To
BETTIANE
the source of all
that matters

AUTHOR'S NOTE

The Spoilers is for the most part a true story. In 1882, San Francisco was the wildest, the wickedest, and certainly the most dangerous city in the West. The cowtowns and mining camps, by comparison, were tame stuff. Host to the Barbary Coast and Chinatown, not to mention a waterfront steeped in infamy, the city by the bay was a cosmopolitan hellhole. In that day and time, it was considered the roughest, and by far the most depraved, metropolis on the North American Continent.

Yet, during this same era, San Francisco was the premier city of the Old West. A financial center, a place of sophistication and culture, it was already a mythical wonder famed for its natural beauty and idyllic setting. Beneath the surface, however, there was an unholy marriage between underworld vice lords and corrupt politicians. Their alliance, bolstered by savage methods and a callous disregard for human life, was to rule San Francisco for nearly a quarter-century. Their downfall, when it came, happened very much as described in the story that follows.

The characters who people *The Spoilers* are real. Their names are unchanged, and the diabolic manner in which they pillaged San Francisco required no invention. Some license has been taken with events and dates, but the spoilers themselves are, if anything, less formidable than they were in real life. Luke Starbuck represents a breed apart. A detective and manhunter, he relied on wits and guts, and when necessary, a fast gun. His assignment in *The Spoilers* borders more on fact than fiction.

Chapter One

A brisk October wind swept across the bay. The ferry plowed toward San Francisco, buffeted by the choppy waters. Directly ahead lay the waterfront, a sprawling collection of wharves and warehouses below the hill-studded city.

Luke Starbuck stood alone at the railing on the bow. The other passengers, crossing on the morning ferry from Oakland, were huddled inside the warmth of the main-deck cabin. Face to the wind, Starbuck appeared heedless of the damp chill and the spray that peppered him as waves slapped against the hull. His eyes were fixed on the harbor and the city beyond. He thought it the damnedest sight he'd ever seen.

Telegraph Hill, towering prominently above the waterfront, was cloaked in fog. Around the curving shore of the bay, the terrain formed a bold amphitheater, with inland hills surrounding the center of the city. The bay itself, perhaps the finest landlocked harbor in the world, was crowded with ships. At anchor were vessels of all nations, mast upon mast, their flags fluttering in the breeze. Westward, hidden by the fog-bound peninsula, was the Golden Gate. Through its channel, and into the harbor, sailed the ships of the China trade. Their cargo holds were filled with copra and raw silk, coconut oil and sugar, and myriad imports from the exotic Orient. The trade had transformed San Francisco into one of the richest ports on earth.

To Starbuck, who was not easily impressed, it was grander than anything he'd imagined. A former cowhand and rancher, he had grown to manhood in the Texas Panhandle. Circumstance had thrust him into the role of range detective, and several years were spent in the employ of Cattlemen's Associations across the West. As his reputation grew, he'd been hired by diverse organizations, like banks and mining companies. He was known to have killed at least twenty men, and among outlaws, he was considered the deadliest of all manhunters. Yet his skill as a detective by far exceeded his renown with a gun. His services were in constant demand, and though he was something of a lone wolf, his credentials were on a level with those of the Pinkerton Agency. He was celebrated as a man who never quit, that rare blend of bulldog and bloodhound. He got results.

For all his experience, however, Starbuck was not widely traveled. His work had been confined primarily to the Rocky Mountains and the Southern Plains. To him, Denver was a metropolis, and any body of water wider than the Rio Grande was beyond his ken. The sight of the bay, with tall-masted clippers and ocean-going steamers, was therefore a marvel to command attention. San Francisco, wonderously situated in a ring of hills, and several times the size of Denver, was like a storybook come to life. A profusion of cultures, cosmopolitan and sophisticated, it was the premier city of the West.

Watching it from the bow of the ferry, Starbuck felt a keen sense of exhilaration, and a quickening excitement. He told himself he'd been wise to accept Charles Crocker's summons. Whether or not he accepted the assignment was another thing, and suddenly not too important. Simply being here—San Francisco itself—was well worth the trip. He thought he might stay a while.

Only a week before, he'd been on the verge of accepting another assignment from Wells, Fargo. Then, out of the blue, he had received a wire from Charles Crocker, president of the Central Pacific Railroad. The message was terse, lacking specifics, but urgent in tone. Crocker requested Starbuck's presence in San Frencisco, stressing the need for his professional services, and offered to pay all expenses.

Headquartered in Denver, Starbuck had never been retained by a railroad, and the idea intrigued him. He wired an affirmative reply and caught the next westbound. Arriving in Oakland yesterday evening, he had spent the night in a lodging house. Crocker's summons had indicated no need for secrecy, but by now it was second nature. He was entering San Francisco unknown and unannounced, one of the crowd.

When the ferry docked, he was the first to step ashore. He walked along the wharf and stopped on the corner of Market Street. The main thoroughfare of the city, Market began at the waterfront and bisected the business district. He stood for a moment, feeling somewhat like a hayseed, and simply stared. There was no question that San Francisco put Denver to shame. The buildings were taller. The people were more fashionably dressed, and crowded the sidewalks in greater numbers. There was a greater profusion of carriages and hansom cabs, blocking the street as far as the eye could see. The clamor and hubbub were deafening, and the whole scene put him in mind of an ant heap busily swarming with activity. Everything was bigger and louder, and somehow larger than life. He suddenly understood why the city by the bay was spoken of in awed terms.

Still, nothing daunted Starbuck for long. He took it all in stride, and quickly decided there was no reason to gawk. People were people, and ant heaps were all much alike, some merely larger and louder than others. Stepping off the corner, he dodged in front of a carriage and hopped aboard a horse-drawn streetcar. He paid his fare, asking the conductor for directions, and found a seat in the rear. Several blocks uptown, he spotted the triangle where Montgomery and Post intersected Market, and jumped down. He joined the crowd and walked north along Montgomery.

Crossing Sutter, he saw the Wells, Fargo Building kitty-corner across the street. He was tempted to step inside and pay his respects. Only four months ago, while working undercover for the stage company, he had been instrumental in running Wyatt Earp out of Arizona. With Earp's departure, stagecoach robbery in the Tombstone district had all but ceased. The company had awarded Starbuck a generous bonus for his part in routing the gang. Now, however, he resisted the impulse to stop by Wells, Fargo. He wasn't a tactful man, but neither was he a dimdot. Having hedged on accepting a new assignment, it wouldn't do to let them know he was in town to see Crocker. Wells, Fargo could wait.

At the next corner, in the heart of the financial district, he found the Mills Building. The corporate offices of the Central Pacific Railroad occupied the entire third floor. A rickety elevator deposited him in the waiting room, and he gave his name to a man seated behind a reception desk. An office boy scurried off to announce his arrival, and he took a chair. Several minutes later, a young man with thick glasses approached, introducing himself as Crocker's secretary. He led Starbuck down a long hallway and ushered him into a corner suite.

Charles Crocker's office was lavishly appointed. Overlooking the intersection of Montgomery and Bush, it was furnished with wing chairs and a sofa crafted in lush Moroccan leather. The floor was covered by an immense Persian carpet and the walls were lined with oil paintings of the California coast. At the far end of the room, framed between two windows, was a gargantuan desk that looked to be carved from a solid piece of teak. The room seemed somehow appropriate to the man who rose from behind the desk.

Starbuck was reminded of a whale. Charles Crocker topped six feet and weighed not a stone less than three hundred pounds. Age had begun to thicken his girth, and his muttonchop beard was flecked through with gray. Yet he moved with vigor and held himself in a posture of ramrod self-assurance that bordered on arrogance. His voice was deep and resonant, with a booming, organ-like quality.

"Welcome, Mr. Starbuck!" He extended an arm the size of a log. "Welcome to San Francisco."

"Mr. Crocker." Starbuck found his handshake only slightly less powerful than a bear trap. "Glad to be here."

"How was your trip?"

"No complaints. You run a pretty fair railroad."

"None better!" Crocker said affably, waving him to a chair. "We pride ourselves on that. Indeed, we do!"

Starbuck seated himself in one of the wing chairs. The secretary, without being asked, took the other chair. Adjusting his glasses, he pulled a pad and pencil from his pocket, and waited at stiff-backed attention. Crocker crossed behind the desk and lowered his bulk into a tall swivel chair.

"Well, now," he said in his orotund voice, "down to business. You haven't come all this way for chitchat, correct, Mr. Starbuck?"

"I'm all ears, Mr. Crocker. Fire away."

"Excellent!" Crocker gestured toward his secretary. "I'll just have Higgins take notes on our discussion. For the record, so to speak."

"Why do you need a record?"

"Standard practice," Crocker explained. "I trust you have no objection?"

Starbuck looked at him without expression. "I'm not much for talking on the record."

"May I ask why?"

"Things put down on paper sometimes come back to haunt you."

"Aren't you being overly cautious, Mr. Starbuck?"

"We all protect ourselves in different ways."

"Indeed?" Crocker said gruffly. "Well, suffice it to say, I never enter into an arrangement without a written record."

"Your privilege," Starbuck remarked in a dry, cold manner. "I never make a deal in writing. A handshake does it, or it doesn't get done."

"Suppose I break my word, decide not to pay you when the assignment's completed?"

Starbuck gave him a slow, dark smile. "You won't."

Starbuck was a rock of a man. He was sledge-shouldered, with lithe catlike reflexes, and taller than he appeared. His hair was sandy colored and his pale blue eyes took another man's measure in one swift glance. His gaze, now centered on Crocker, was steady and confident. The result was striking, somehow cold and very impersonal.

Crocker met and held his gaze. He was aware he'd underestimated the younger man. From all reports, Starbuck was a crackerjack detective; but those same reports indicated he was a mankiller, devoid of compassion or mercy when pushed beyond certain limits. After a moment's reflection, he was forced to admit Starbuck had a point. Today they wouldn't be dealing in vague abstractions. Their discussion, by necessity, would touch on the subject of death. That was something better left out of the record. A handshake would do very nicely.

"That's all, Higgins." He dismissed the secretary with a curt nod. "I'll call if I need you."

Higgins rose, looking slightly bemused, and walked from the room. There was a long, strained silence until the door closed. Then Crocker leaned back in the swivel chair, which creaked ominously under his weight.

"You're a cool one, Mr. Starbuck."

"No offense," Starbuck said woodenly. "A man in my line of work can't afford to take chances."

"I daresay," Crocker agreed, quickly moving on. "Now, as to the reason I asked you here. The Central Pacific has a problem with train robbers. I want it stopped."

"How serious a problem?"

"Very close to ruinous, Mr. Starbuck. Our express cars carry gold from the San Francisco mint and currency shipments from the banks throughout California. Over the past year we've been robbed on an average of twice a month. The losses, as you may well appreciate, have been staggering."

"No idea who's behind it?"

"None."

"The same gang every time?"

"We think so, but there's no way of knowing for certain."

"Any pattern?" Starbuck ventured. "Do they favor a certain section of the line? Or maybe strike at a certain time of the month?"

"Yes to both questions. More often than not they raid the southern line, somewhere between here and San Jose. As to timing, they *always* strike when we're carrying a large shipment."

"Always?" Starbuck regarded him with impassive curiosity. "Are you saying they know exactly which trains to hit?"

"I am, indeed," Crocker said in an aggrieved tone. "That's why I summoned you, Mr. Starbuck. We have a Judas in our midst—someone who supplies them with our shipment schedules. No matter what precautions we take—despite the utmost secrecy—they always know. Always!"

Starbuck's eyes were hard, questing. "What about your own security force? With the pattern established, they could've pulled a switch and waylaid the robbers."

Crocker looked painfully embarrassed. "We tried that on two separate occasions. In both instances, the train wasn't robbed."

"Your Judas tipped them off in advance?"

"Precisely."

"So you're asking me to ferret out the Judas?"

"The Judas," Crocker said, watching him carefully, "and the gang leader. I want it stopped—permanently."

A stony look settled on Starbuck's face. He'd heard the same message many times before. Always phrased discreetly, never in the form of a direct order, it was nonetheless obvious. Someone needed to be killed, and he was being asked to do the job. He gave Crocker an evaluating glance, then shrugged.

"I work at my own speed and I do it my own way. If I take the assignment, then I'll report directly to you and no one else."

"Does that include Tom Kelly, our security chief?"

"That includes everybody and anyone. Either our meeting today stays inside these four walls or I want no part of the deal. One little hint, and your Judas would most likely punch my ticket."

"Where would you begin?"

"Where it's least expected," Starbuck said stolidly. "I'll let you know after I've had a chance to nose around."

Crocker's expression was speculative. "How would you report to me?"

"Never here," Starbuck told him firmly. "I'll figure a way to get word to you. If it's necessary that we meet, then it'll have to be somewhere else. Somewhere damn private, and always by yourself."

"In other words, you would operate independently and keep me informed as it suits your pleasure. Is that essentially correct?"

"That's the way I work," Starbuck said levelly. "So far it's kept me alive."

"An admirable record," Crocker observed with a tinge of irony. "Now, as to your fee. I presume you have a standard rate?"

Starbuck had done his homework on the Central Pacific. In 1862, two companies were awarded federal charters to build a transcontinental railroad: the Union Pacific, building westward from the Missouri River, and the Central Pacific, building eastward from California. Crocker and three business cronies—Leland Stanford, Mark Hopkins, and Collis Huntington—were the sole stockholders of the Central Pacific. Thereafter, they were known as the Big Four, and with reason. The government granted them nine million acres of land, $24,000,000 in federal bonds, and no strings attached. For four years, three thousand Irishmen and ten thousand Chinese coolies labored to build their railroad. One of the end results was San Francisco's fabled Chinatown. The other was a separate construction company, which had exclusive rights to purchase material and build the Central Pacific. Crocker and his cohorts, once again the sole stockholders, raised $79,000,000 in bonds and cash from the government and private investors. Of that amount, $36,000,000, not counting river frontage and ocean property, was siphoned off into their own pockets. The facts had slowly come to light, and now, in 1882, the holdings of the Big Four were conservatively estimated at $100,000,000 or more.

The newspapers of the day, never overly fond of robber barons, had characterized Crocker as "ruthless as a crocodile" and a man who believed in "the brute force of money." Having briefed himself on the Big Four in general, and Crocker in particular, Starbuck saw no reason to be charitable. He had come to the meeting fully prepared to deal with a crocodile, and he hadn't been disappointed. Then, too, having heard the assignment, he now had fewer qualms about holding Crocker's feet to the fire.

"One hundred dollars a day," Starbuck said at length. "All expenses paid and a minimum guarantee of a thousand dollars. That's my standard rate."

"Awfully steep, isn't it?" Crocker complained. "The Pinkerton Agency only charges half that amount."

"The Pinkertons won't do the job you want done, otherwise you would've hired them to start with."

"I'm afraid I don't follow you."

"It's simple enough," Starbuck said in a deliberate voice. "You want your Judas and the gang leader killed.

No arrest, no trial, just a couple of quick funerals and the less fanfare the better."

"I didn't say that."

"Naturally." Starbuck cracked a smile. "If you had to say it, then I'd be the wrong man for the job. Tell me it's not so and I'll head on back to Denver."

Crocker gave him a faint nod of satisfaction. "Your terms are acceptable."

"I'll be in touch."

Starbuck heaved himself to his feet. Crocker rose and they shook hands, staring gravely into each other's eyes. Then, with no parting word, Starbuck turned and walked out. He closed the door softly behind him.

Crocker slumped back into his chair. His palms were sweaty, and he breathed a heavy sigh of relief. There for a moment, looking into Starbuck's eyes, he had experienced the sensation of fear. He knew it was justified, and he felt no shame.

He had the distinct impression he'd just struck a bargain with the Devil himself.

Chapter Two

Starbuck arrived at the depot shortly before boarding time.

The morning train for Los Angeles departed at seven o'clock, and by his watch he had a quarter-hour to spare. He purchased a ticket for Salinas, then crossed the waiting room to the departure gate. He carried no luggage, but he was nonetheless prepared to travel. A Colt sixgun, hidden by his suit jacket, rode comfortably in a crossdraw holster.

Outside, he paused on the platform and pulled out the makings. He creased the paper, sprinkling tobacco, and rolled himself a smoke. A flick of his thumbnail struck a match and he lit the cigarette. Moving to one side, he propped himself up against a wall, quietly watchful. His eyes slowly scanned the crowded platform.

The San Francisco-to-Los Angeles run was clearly profitable. A large throng of passengers had already boarded, and others were saying their last goodbyes to family and well-wishers. Everyone looked perfectly ordinary, businessmen and drummers, working stiffs and farmers, and a dithering assortment of women and children. None of them appeared to be packing a gun, and there wasn't a suspicious face in the crowd. Insofar as he could determine, it was simply another day on the Central Pacific. Nothing out of place, no reason for alarm.

His attention moved to the train itself. There were four passenger coaches, normal for the morning run to Los Angeles. Down the line, the locomotive chuffed and belched steam. The tender was freshly loaded with coal, and directly behind, the last of the mail sacks were being loaded aboard the express car. A mail sorter and two guards, both armed with pistols, were visible through the door. Coupled to the rear of the train was a slat-sided boxcar. While unusual, for livestock was normally hauled by freight trains, its presence today was wholly unavoidable. The boxcar was part and parcel of Starbuck's plan.

On the platform, near the open door of the boxcar, a man stood smoking a pipe. He was tall and lanky, almost cadaverous in appearance, and he wore the rough-garbed clothing of a stockman. He was watching the crowd with no apparent interest, puffing cottony wads of smoke. His manner was somewhat resigned, almost bored. The look of a hired hand stuck with an unpleasant chore.

Starbuck sauntered over, the cigarette stuck in the corner of his mouth. He stopped in front of the man, nodding amiably.

"Howdy."

"Mornin'," the man replied. "Do something for you?"

"Well, neighbor, my curiosity's workin' overtime.

Thought mebbe you'd oblige me by answerin' a question."

Starbuck easily slipped into the lingo of the range. His boots and wide-brimmed hat, the roll-your-own dangling from his lips, all did the trick. The man brightened and responded in the slow drawl common to south Texas.

"You're a long ways from home, ain't you?"

"For a fact," Starbuck grinned. "Hail from the Panhandle, couple of days ride north of San Angelo."

"Damnation! Ain't that one for the books! I'm from down around Laredo myself."

"Pegged you for a Texican! Yessir, I was standin' over there and I says to myself, that feller's got the look of homefolks. Figgered I'd just mosey over and see."

"Glad you did! Shore good to hear a man speak plain English again."

Starbuck held out his hand. "Name's Joe Dobbs."

"Hank Noonan." After pumping his arm, Noonan gave him a quizzical look. "What brings you out here?"

"Aww, just rubber-neckin'," Starbuck chuckled. "Fell into a little *dinero* and thought I'd take a gander at the ocean. Never seen one a'fore." He paused, took a drag on his cigarette. "What about your ownself?"

"Horse trainer." Noonan puffed importantly on his pipe. "Feller name of Crocker—owns this here very railroad—come down to the King spread a few years back and bought hisself a string of thoroughbreds. I was head wrangler there at the time and he hired me to wetnurse his stock. Been out here ever since."

"Got a nice outfit, does he?"

"Fair to middlin'," Noonan allowed. "Thousand acres or so down along the coast. But he's got an eye for racehorses, and the pay's good too."

"That's what got my curiosity whetted. Wondered why they had a stockcar hooked onto a passenger train."

"Have a looksee." Noonan jerked a thumb at the boxcar. "Takin' one of Crocker's mares down to a breedin' farm in the San Joaquin Valley. Him ownin' the railroad, he can pretty damn much do what he pleases. That's how come she wasn't put on a regular freight run."

Starbuck crushed his cigarette underfoot, then stuck his head through the boxcar door. A chestnut mare, haltered and tied in a stall, stood munching hay. His gaze shifted quickly around the car and abruptly stopped. He spotted an old saddle and some bridle gear piled near a water barrel. He grunted softly to himself, satisfied.

"Aboard! All aboard!"

The conductor's voice rang out in a last call to passengers. Starbuck turned, clapping Noonan on the shoulder, and gave him a parting handshake. Then, as the Texan scrambled into the boxcar, he hurried forward. Bypassing the rear coaches, he walked along the platform. The train lurched and he swung aboard the first coach, directly behind the express car. The conductor gave him a dirty look and signaled the engineer. Moments later, the train gathered speed and rolled southward out of the switching yard.

Starbuck found a window seat toward the front of the coach. A sundries drummer was seated beside him, and they passed the next few minutes in idle conversation. Presently, a candy butcher came through hawking sweets and sandwiches. The drummer, commenting he'd missed breakfast, bought a ham and cheese that looked stale as sawdust. Then the conductor passed by, punching tickets, and announced an upcoming stop. Starbuck yawned a wide jaw-cracking yawn, and settled deeper into his seat. He pulled his hat down over his eyes, and left the drummer to his sandwich.

Feigning sleep, he mentally reviewed all he'd learned over the past three days. Even now, he was looking for holes in his plan, something he might have missed. However careful, no man was infallable. He'd made mistakes before, and he would likely make some this trip out. But in his view, that was no excuse for sloppy planning. He especially wanted no miscues today.

After his meeting with Crocker, he had holed up in a seedy Mission District hotel. There, sprawled out on the bed, he had analyzed the various approaches he might take. On balance, he'd concluded that the place to start was with the robbers themselves. To go undercover within Central Pacific would have proved time-consuming, and perhaps not all that productive. The railroad's organization—the sheer number of people—was simply too vast and too segmented. It would have taken him weeks, maybe even months, to establish himself and work his way through the organization. The time span might have been shortened by limiting himself to upper-echelon departments; but that approach had serious drawbacks, as well. There were too many people, from clerks to vice-presidents, with access to express-car shipment schedules. And the Judas, obviously a slippery customer, would not be caught napping.

All in all, it seemed to Starbuck that the fastest and most direct aproach was the gang itself. Once he identified the ringleader, and had him under surveillance, it wouldn't take long to isolate the Judas. Barring that, he could, as a last resort, pass himself off as a hardcase and infiltrate the gang. He'd done it with cattle rustlers and stage robbers, and he had no doubt it would work with train robbers. Yet that, too, would consume time—perhaps a month or longer—for outlaws were slow to accept a stranger into their ranks. By far, the better plan was to let the gang leader lay a trail to the Judas. Then, in a manner of speaking, he would kill two birds with one stone. Or at the very least, a couple of .45 slugs.

That much decided, Starbuck had contacted Crocker the next evening, slipping unobstrusively into his mansion on Nob Hill. He obtained a map of the Central Pacific railway lines and pinpointed the exact location of all previous robberies. A detailed study of the map proved illuminating. While a few of the holdups had occurred on the run to Sacramento, the majority had taken place in the fifty-mile stretch between San Francisco and the Santa Cruz Mountains. He put himself in the robbers' boots—a feat of mental gymnastics he'd learned as a manhunter—and arrived at a gut-certain hunch. The gang was quite probably operating from a hideout within a twenty-mile radius of Los Altos, a sleepy whistlestop some thirty miles south of San Francisco. Telegraph had improved communications among law officers, and the gang leader was clearly no dimwit. After pulling a holdup, the robbers had never been sighted, much less pursued. That strongly indicated they had a hideout that was within two hours' ride of the jobs they'd pulled to date. He determined that the first step was to unearth their hideout.

The following night he had again contacted Crocker and outlined his plan. An unusually large express shipment was to be arranged two days hence, on the morning train to Los Angeles. Everything was to appear routine, and standard security measures were to be employed. Crocker had bellyached long and loud, demanding extra guards to prevent loss of the money. Starbuck remained adamant, arguing that the gang must be lured into a holdup and thereby afford him the advantage of a fresh trail. In the end, common sense prevailed and he'd got his way. His last request, more so than the money, had brought on a fit of near apoplexy. Using some plausible cover story, one of Crocker's racehorses was to be shipped south on the same train. A hot shouting match ensued, but in that, too, he had prevailed. He left Crocker to work out the necessary subterfuge.

Now, scrunched down in his seat, he concluded he'd left nothing undone. All was in readiness, and it remained only for the gang to take the bait. Some inner voice told him he wouldn't be disappointed. He closed his eyes and almost instantly, like an animal, he was asleep.

The train passed through Los Altos an hour or so later. Awake and watchful, Starbuck began to wonder if he'd bet a loser. The next stop was San Jose, some twenty miles down the line. The gang, according to the information provided by Crocker, had never robbed a train south of San Jose. Which meant it had to happen soon or not at all.

Long ago, Starbuck had determined that outlaws were essentially lazy. For all their cunning, those who rode the owlhoot were unimaginative and generally possessed more balls than brains. Unlike high-class crooks, such as con men and grifters, the average desperado was a creature of habit. Unwittingly, because he was shiftless and indolent, he took the path of least resistance. Once he stumbled upon a method that worked, he seemed to fall into a rut, seldom attempting anything new or novel. A pattern invariably emerged, and his actions thereafter became somewhat predictable. All of which gave Starbuck reason for concern.

Unless the gang struck soon, his plan would very

likely prove a washout. There was always tomorrow, and another plan, but he much preferred today. He prided himself on outguessing crooks—the first time around.

Starbuck's judgment was vindicated some five miles south of Los Altos. On a dogleg curve, a tree had been felled across the tracks. The engineer set the brakes and the train jarred to a screeching halt. The sudden jolt caught the passengers unawares, and there was a moment of pandemonium in the coaches. Women screamed and men cursed, and luggage from the overhead racks went flying down the aisle. Untangling themselves, the passengers were dazed and not a little fearful. Their voices verged on panic.

Then, suddenly, a collective hush fell over the coaches. A gang of masked riders burst out of the woods bordering the tracks. Four men rode directly to the express car, pouring a volley of shots through the door. The three remaining men, spurring their horses hard, charged up and down the track bed. Their pistols were cocked and pointed at the passengers, who stared open-mouthed through the coach windows. No shots were fired, but the message was clear: *Stay on the train or get killed.* Which made eminent good sense to the passengers. The Central Pacific, like most railroads, was not revered by the public. A holdup, according to common wisdom, was a matter between the railroad and the bandits. Only a fool would risk his life for the likes of the Big Four. And there were no fools aboard today.

Starbuck had a ringside seat. From his position in the front of the coach, the four men outside the express car were plainly visible. Watching them, he had to admire their no-nonsense approach to train robbery. One of the riders produced a stick of dynamite and held the fuse only inches away from the tip of a lighted cigar. Another rider, his voice raised in a commanding shout, then informed the express guards that they had a choice: *Open the door or get blown to Kingdom Come!*

The guards, much like the passengers, were unwilling to die for the Central Pacific. The door slid open and the guards dutifully tossed their pistols onto the track bed. Three of the robbers dismounted and clambered inside the express car. The other three, still menacing the passengers with pointed guns, held their positions outside the coaches. The seventh man, the one with the foghorn voice, directed the operation from aboard his horse. His tone had the ring of authority, brusque and demanding. His attitude was that of a man accustomed to being obeyed.

Starbuck immediately tagged him as the gang leader. He looked to be of medium height, powerfully built, and he was dressed in the nondescript workclothes worn by the other men. A slouch hat covered his head, and a wide bandanna, pulled up over his nose, effectively masked his features. Yet, upon closer observation, Starbuck spotted something that couldn't be hidden. A thatch of red hair, brilliant orangy-red, spilled out from beneath the slouch hat. Bright as a sunset, it was a head of hair that would stand out in any crowd.

From start to finish, the holdup took less than five minutes. The robbers inside the express car emerged with mail sacks stuffed full of cash and quickly mounted their horses. On signal from their leader, the gang opened fire and raked the length of the train with a barrage of lead. The shots were purposely placed high, but windows shattered and wall panels splintered and the angry snarl of bullets ripped through the coaches. Everyone dove for the floor and prudently stayed there. A moment later the gunfire ceased and the thud of hoofbeats drummed the earth.

Starbuck peeked over the windowsill just as the gang disappeared into the woods. He jumped to his feet, hopping over the drummer, and moved through the door. Outside, he went down the coach steps and sprinted toward the rear of the train. Not ten seconds elapsed from the last gunshot to the time he pulled up in front of the boxcar. He hammered on the door with his fist.

"Noonan! Hank Noonan! Open up!"

"Who's there?"

"Joe Dobbs! C'mon, get the lead out! It's life or death!"

"Hold on, Joe!" The door flew open and Noonan gaped down at him with a look of fright. "Lord God A'mighty, they didn't shoot you, did—"

Starbuck showed him a cocked sixgun. "Hank, I want you to listen real close and do exactly what I say. Savvy?"

Noonan bobbed his head, eyes popped out like a pair of fried eggs. Following Starbuck's instructions, he muscled the loading ramp to the door and dropped it into place. Starbuck climbed inside, noting out of the corner of his eye that a crowd of men had gathered around the express car. He ordered Noonan to saddle the mare. The Texan suddenly pulled up, his features twisted in a mulish frown.

"No sir!" he muttered hotly. "You ain't gonna steal—"

Starbuck wagged the snout of the sixgun. "Don't play hero, *compadre*. Just get it done—*muy pronto!*"

Grumbling under his breath, Noonan went to work. He saddled the mare, afterward fitting the bit into her mouth and slipping the bridle over her head. Then he backed her out of the stall and walked her to the door.

With an unpleasant grunt, he tossed the reins to Starbuck.

"I dunno your game, but you shore picked the wrong horse. Old man Crocker's gonna hang your ass a mile high."

"Obliged for the warning, Hank. Now step aside and don't make any sudden moves."

Starbuck holstered his gun and looped the reins around the mare's neck. He stepped into the saddle, tugged at the brim of his hat, and gave Noonan a sardonic smile. Then he feathered the mare in the ribs and reined her down the loading ramp. Once clear of the track bed, he gigged her hard and rode off at a gallop.

A moment later he vanished into the trees.

Chapter Three

The chase lasted almost three hours.

From the outset, it was apparent to Starbuck that he'd underestimated the gang leader. He had expected a furious dash, speed rather than deception. That view had been reinforced when the job was pulled scarcely five miles south of Los Altos. An hour's hard ride, on a direct beeline to the hideout, was how he had visualized it upon taking the trail. He'd never been more wrong.

Instead of a beeline, the robbers zigzagged all over the countryside. A mile or so north of the holdup scene, they suddenly changed course and circled west of Los Altos. In the process, they crisscrossed several creeks, and at one point held their horses to mid-stream for something more than a half-mile. Then they switched directions and again turned due north. Their path, however, was meandering and uncannily deceptive.

At all times, the gang warily avoided open ground. While they never doubled back, they stuck to redwood forests and scrub-choked hills wherever possible. Upon encountering lowlands, they veered off into rocky defiles latticed with brushy undergrowth. Their general direction was always north, but the winding route followed a network of harsh and seemingly predetermined obstacles. Quite clearly, they knew the terrain and had developed evasive stratagems to throw off pursuit. To all but a skilled tracker, their trail would have been lost within a few miles.

Starbuck's years as a manhunter served him well. Early on in his career, he had worked solely as a range detective. His principal targets were cattle rustlers and horse thieves, men schooled in plains lore and the artful dodges of hiding a trail. By necessity, he had become a tracker of surpassing skill, able to read signs practically invisible to the naked eye. Today, those skills permitted him to follow a crazy-quilt path that would have defeated ordinary lawmen. Several times he lost sight of the gang, but he never lost their trail. He stuck to their tracks like a born Apache.

An hour into the chase Starbuck realized he had committed another error. Having underestimated the gang leader, he had thoughtlessly compounded the problem by choosing the wrong mount. The thoroughbred mare was built for speed, not endurance. Unlike common saddle horses, she had no bottom, no staying power over the long haul. North of Los Altos she began to play out, and he had no choice but to conserve her stamina. His pace was slowed even further, and with each passing mile, he found himself falling farther behind. Once again, his ability to read sign and track on hard ground kept him in the race.

Yet, for all his skill, he barely avoided disaster in the end. Shortly after midday, he was tracking through a low range of mountains. His eyes were on broken twigs and crushed vegetation, and the sign indicated he was perhaps twenty minutes behind the gang. He topped a ridge, and spread out before him the mountains dropped off to a rolling plain. At the bottom of the ridge was a creek, bordered by trees, and on the far side was a farmhouse and a small barn. For a moment, looking down with surprise, nothing registered. Then he saw the corral, and the horses. And gathered outside the farmhouse, a group of men.

Suddenly it dawned on him that he was skylined. Wondering if he'd been seen, he sawed at the reins and whipped the mare back over the ridge. A short distance north, he dismounted and left the mare tied in a grove of trees. He walked quickly to the ridge, removing his hat, and went belly down. Below, not a hundred yards away, he had a commanding view of the farmhouse. The men were still bunched near the front door, and there was no apparent sign of alarm. He thought it was his lucky day. Goddamned lucky!

A closer look confirmed that the chase had indeed ended. He spotted the red-haired gang leader, clearly a standout even at a distance. The men were gathered around a water pump, taking turns sluicing off the grime of a long and dusty ride. Apparently in good humor, their leader was gesturing and talking in a loud voice. The sound of laughter carried distinctly to the ridge top.

Starbuck's attention was abruptly drawn to the corral. He saw a man, dressed in bib overalls, forking hay to the horses. A quick count verified that he was not one of the original seven who had robbed the train. Upon closer inspection, Starbuck realized there was more to the farm than he'd seen at first glance. Beyond the house, several acres were fenced and planted with a variety of vegetables. Off in the distance, a herd of some twenty dairy cows grazed placidly in the noonday sun. No hardscrabble operation, the farm had a look of substance and prosperity. The abundance of produce, and the presence of milk cows, meant only one thing. There was a marketplace nearby, probably no more than a few hours' ride way.

A woman suddenly stepped through the doorway of the house and called to the men. She wore a checkered apron, and from her scolding manner, Starbuck sensed she was summoning the men to a hot meal. For the first time, he noticed the mail sacks piled beside the door. As the gang trooped inside, the burly redhead and another man each hefted one of the sacks. From all appearances, more than a hot meal would be divvied up over the dinner table.

Something bothered Starbuck about the setup. A dairy farmer and his wife seemed unlikely accomplices for a band of train robbers. Nor was the farm itself the hideout he'd expected to find. One somehow didn't dovetail with the other.

The thought prompted another question. He wondered where the hell he was. He had some general idea, for he knew the chase had carried him far north of Los Altos. But he had no notion of where it had ended, or exactly how far north.

He pulled the map from his inside coat pocket and spread it on the ground. Turning, he studied the mountain range, noting rises in elevation and dominant peaks. With one eye on the terrain, he slowly scanned the map. Suddenly he blinked and his finger jabbed at a spot that marked the flatland below. The farm was on the western slope of the San Bruno Mountains, roughly in the center of the peninsula. The hairpin bend in the creek pinpointed his precise location.

He was less than ten miles south of San Francisco.

The sheer audacity of it was stunning. No one would believe a gang of train robbers would operate that close to a major city. Nor would anyone suspect that a tranquil dairy farm was an outlaw hideout. It took the cake for nerve, and it proved that there was always an exception to any rule. The red-haired gang leader not only had a big set of balls; he had brains, as well. The whole operation had been planned with a sort of tactical genius.

On impulse, Starbuck was struck by another of his hunches. The farmhouse was a rendezvous, not a hideout. A meeting place and a way station for the horses. A stopover for the gang before they rode on to somewhere else.

He smiled, nodding to himself, and returned the map to his coat pocket. Then he settled down to wait.

A short time later Starbuck got still another surprise. The train robbers, followed by the farmer, emerged from the house. Yet they were now an altogether different group of men. Their workclothes had been exchanged for city suits and bowler hats; the transformation was startling. No longer was there any resemblance to the gang that had stopped the morning train.

The barn doors were opened and two carriages were rolled outside. A team of bays and a team of chestnuts were then led from the barn and hitched to the carriages. Four men climbed aboard the first carriage and took off along a wagon trail that snaked westward. The gang leader and the others waited, talking quietly amongst themselves, until some ten minutes had passed. Then they stepped into the second carriage, waving to the farmer, and drove off in the same direction. To all appearances, they might have been businessmen or land speculators, or even a crew of Bible salesmen canvassing the countryside. By no stretch of the imagination would anyone connect them to the train holdup.

Starbuck quickly checked his map. He located the wagon trail and saw that it intersected a main road, running north-south along the peninsula. The only other road, some miles to the west, skirted the coastline. There were fishing villages along the ocean, and a few small settlements dotted the bay side of the peninsula; all the land in between appeared to be sparsely populated, mainly farms. The relative isolation of the area merely enhanced his respect for the gang. Their rendezvous point, though close to San Francisco, was nonetheless remote. The concept was masterful and the execution flawless. The work of a man who knew his business, a professional.

Waiting until the carriage was out of sight, Starbuck mounted the mare and rode north. He forded the stream a mile or so above the farmhouse, then turned due west. Presently he crested a rise of ground and spotted the main road. He walked the mare to a grove of trees, staying hidden in the shadows, and rolled himself a smoke. Before he had time to finish his cigarette, the carriage appeared from the south. The gang's destination, much as he'd suspected, was San Francisco. Allowing them a five-minute lead, he left the trees and reined the mare toward the road.

He easily kept the carriage in sight.

Once inside the city limits, Starbuck was able to close the gap. By then it was late afternoon, and he was just another horseman on streets clogged with traffic. He had no fixed plan in mind, but he'd set himself a task that was essential to any further action. Before the night was out, he meant to establish the gang leader's identity.

The carriage led him across town, to the intersection of Jackson and Sansome. There, the team and carriage were dropped off at a livery stable. He dismounted, hitching the mare outside a saloon on the opposite corner. The four men in the first carriage were nowhere in evidence, but that gave him no reason for concern. After a robbery, very likely wearing money belts stuffed with cash, it figured they would scatter. Shortly, the thought was confirmed when the burly redhead talked with the two men a moment, then waved and walked off. He turned north on Sansome.

Starbuck followed, strolling casually along the opposite side of the street. The sidewalks were thronged with passersby, and he readily blended into the crowd. Having spent three days in San Francisco, he'd gotten his bearings, and the direction of the surveillance came as no great surprise. The gang leader was moving at a brisk pace toward the Barbary Coast.

A hellhole, infamous throughout the world, the Barbary Coast was not for those of faint heart. On the bay side, it was bounded by the waterfront and Telegraph Hill, and extended several blocks inland along Pacific and Broadway streets. A wild carnival of depravity and crime, the area was devoted to dancehalls and brothels, gambling casinos and groggeries, and sinister crimping joints where sailors were drugged and shanghaied for brutal voyages at sea. Vice and debauchery were the district's stock-in-trade.

Local legend attributed the name to the African coastline of earlier notoriety. Whatever its ancestory, the Barbary Coast transformed the dreams of sailors and landlubbers alike into wicked, and sometimes deadly, reality. On average, there were several murders a night, with seamen the most common victims. After voyages lasting two to four years, the sailors were ripe for women, alcohol, and some of the gamier pursuits known to man. The Opera Comique, a dive billing carnal entertainment, presented live shows involving feats of copulation that ranged from acrobatic couples to onstage orgies. Not to be outdone, the Boar's Head staged a show-stopper in which the buxom star was mated on alternate nights to a shetland pony and bull mastiff. No man, however low his tastes, failed to get his money's worth on the Barbary Coast.

Starbuck trailed the gang leader to the Bella Union. A somewhat higher-class establishment, it was located at an intersection humorously dubbed Murder Corner. Offering all things to all men, it provided women, gaming tables, and risqué stage shows. A billboard out front ballyhooed the attractions inside:

PLAIN TALK AND BEAUTIFUL GIRLS!
Lovely Tresses! Lovely Lips! Buxom Forms!
At the
BELLA UNION.
And Such Fun!
If You Don't Want to Risk Both Optics
SHUT ONE EYE.

The batwing doors opened onto a large barroom and gaming parlor. Beyond the bar was a spacious theater, with an orchestra pit and a stage ablaze with footlights. The floor was jammed with tables, and a horseshoe balcony was partitioned into ornate, curtained boxes. Songs and dances were performed, pandering to the profane nature of the clientele, and the atmosphere fell somewhere between licentious and obscene. After their acts, the girls mingled with the customers in a crush of jiggling breasts and fruity buttocks. The sofas in the boxes were reserved for private entertainment, and along with the mandatory bottle of champagne, added greatly to the income of all concerned. A pretty little *danseuse* from the show went for a ten spot, and chilled bubbly doubled the tab. The girl kept half the charge for her services and the balance went to the house.

Sunset was still an hour away, but the Bella Union was already jam-packed. Starbuck shouldered a place at the bar, wedging himself in between a bowlegged sailor and a whiskery miner. He ordered rye and kept one eye on the red-haired robber, who had taken a position at the end of the bar. A close-up look revealed that the man was ugly as a toad, with pockmarked features, nut-brown eyes, and freckles almost the exact color of his hair. Starbuck committed his face to memory.

So far the gang leader had spoken to no one but the bartender. He stood with his elbows hooked over the counter and watched the show with a vacant expression. Onstage, a screeching troupe of dancers was romping through a version of the French *can-can*. Their frilly drawers and black mesh stockings exploded into view as they went into the finale and flung themselves rump first to the floor in *la split*. Then, screaming and tossing their skirts, they leaped to their feet and raced offstage as the curtain dropped. The spectators rewarded them with thunderous applause, which prompted a caterwauling curtain call. Then, awaiting the next act, everyone went back to drinking.

On his second shot of rye, Starbuck saw the gang leader straighten up and nod to someone pushing through the crowd. The man who joined him was stocky and muscular, with a square, tough face and a handlebar mustache. He was dressed like a dandy and carried himself with the cocky poise of a prizefighter. He spoke to the gang leader, who beamed a wide grin, and rapidly bobbed his head. The transformation in the train robber was immediate, and curiously out of character.

He looked not just respectful, but somehow servile. A hardass bandit suddenly turned boot-licker.

Starbuck signaled for another drink. While the barkeep was pouring, he ducked his chin toward the end of the counter. "Shore wouldn't wanna tangle with that pair."

The barkeep followed his gaze, and chuckled. "You'd sure as Christ regret it if you did, cowboy."

"Why? They somebody special?"

"Well, the one with the mustache is Denny O'Brien. Owns the Bella Union and half the Coast. The other one's Red Ned Adair, and claims he's meaner'n tiger spit. For my money, they both are."

"I don't reckon I'd care to argue it either way."

"You've got lots of company, cowboy."

The barkeep hustled off, and Starbuck silently repeated the names to himself. Then he saw the one named O'Brien turn and walk toward a staircase near the entranceway to the theater. The gang leader downed his drink and quickly followed along. Together, they mounted the stairs and disappeared from view.

Starbuck had a visceral instinct for the truth, some sixth sense for divining what lay beneath the surface. He was suddenly struck by the thought that the operation was bigger than he'd suspected. Quite probably an organized mob, with Denny O'Brien calling the shots and Red Ned Adair pulling the holdups. Something told him it was so, and he'd learned long ago never to go against his instincts.

He decided it was time to go undercover.

Chapter Four

Early the next morning Starbuck set out to explore San Francisco. His knowledge of the city was thus far general, and what he needed now was specifics. Every town, much like a timepiece, had inner working forever hidden to the casual observer. He meant to determine Denny O'Brien's place within the underworld mechanism.

Last night, upon leaving the Bella Union, his thoughts were disjointed and without order. He knew essentially what must be done, but he hadn't yet decided *how* it would be done. With some stealth, he had retrieved the mare and left her tied in the courtyard of Crocker's mansion. All the way back down Nob Hill, he had puzzled over the new turn of events. By the time he reached his hotel, he'd arrived at what seemed a logical first step. Before going undercover, he had to establish who was who on the Barbary Coast, and where the owner of the Bella Union fitted into the larger picture. Only then could he develop a workable approach to Denny O'Brien.

Today, like a wolf prowling unfamiliar territory, he made a personal reconnaissance of downtown San Francisco. The sporting crowd seldom awakened before noon, so he spent the morning on a sightseeing tour. He crisscrossed the Barbary Coast, gaining a sense of direction and a feel for the lay of the land. The seedier dives along the waterfront were of little interest, but the larger establishments, located primarily on Pacific and Broadway, held his attention. These were the joints that competed directly with the Bella Union, and he catalogued them for future reference. In the course of his wanderings, he gave Chinatown a brief once-over, then turned uptown. There, somewhat to his surprise, he found still another vice district. Though tightly contained, and considerably smaller than the Barbary Coast, it had the look of flourishing nightlife. He thought to himself that it merited further investigation.

By noontime, he'd seen enough to satisfy his immediate needs. The saloons were open, and he made his way back to the Barbary Coast. He picked a watering hole directly across from the Bella Union, one with a crowd of heavy drinkers and careless talkers. A schooner of beer entitled him to a free lunch, and he helped himself to cold cuts and cheese from the trencherman's counter. Then he bellied up to the bar and went to work.

A master of subtle interrogation, Starbuck had the knack of engaging total strangers in conversation. He was a good listener, and seemed raptly interested in the other man's opinion. He also played on their vanity, professing ignorance of the subject at hand, and got them to reveal more than they realized. With adroit prompting, he kept them talking and guilefully steered the conversation along the course he'd planned. When they parted, he had drained them dry of information while saying almost nothing about himself. He left them full of boozy good cheer and a profound sense of their own importance.

Before three o'clock, Starbuck had hit four saloons. At each stop he put away several schooners of beer and generously stood drinks for those he gulled into conversation. He talked with bartenders and pimps, gamblers and street-corner grifters, and one old barfly who supplied a wealth of Barbary Coast gossip. When he walked out of the fourth saloon, he had unearthed everything and more he'd hoped to learn. His view of San Francisco's underworld was by no means complete, but he knew who was who and precisely what it was they controlled. And with one possible exception, he had their names.

The city was split into three very distinct areas of vice and crime. There was a fine line of demarcation separating the areas, almost as though the boundaries had been staked and mapped. Curiously, there was no spillover of activities, even though the three areas abutted one another like wedges sliced from a pie. The city government, from the mayor's office down to the corner policeman, turned a blind eye to the whole affair. The payoffs, everyone agreed, had made rich men of those in public service.

Denny O'Brien was the acknowledged boss of the Barbary Coast. Nothing happened without his sanction, and he maintained a squad of plug-uglies to enforce his demands. He collected a percentage off the top, and no operation was too small to escape his attention. Even the lowly crib whores and crimp joints paid tribute.

His counterpart in Chinatown was Fung Jing Toy. A tong leader and supreme vice lord, he ran Chinatown with godlike impunity. His *boo how doy* hatchet men collected fees from all underworld enterprises, including gambling, opium dens, and bordellos. He also extorted protection money from legitimate businesses, using intimidation and threats of violence. Finally, with all his rivals killed or whipped into line, he controlled the market in Chinese slave girls. The trade reportedly did a brisk business with Occidental and Oriental alike.

There remained only the area Starbuck had surveyed late that morning. Known as the Uptown Tenderloin, it was a district reserved for swells and the upper strata of San Francisco society. Theaters and opulent restaurants vied with cabarets and plush gambling casinos for the gentry trade. The nightlife was almost decorous, the only exception being the high-priced parlor houses. Discreet madams and beautiful whores served the monied class with all the attention accorded the master of a harem. A parlor-house whore was the *crème de la crème* of her trade, and a bright girl occasionally snared herself a millionaire. According to those who knew, more than one matron on Nob Hill had begun her career in the Tenderloin.

Yet there was an apparent contradiction to the Uptown Tenderloin. All afternoon Starbuck had tactfully posed the same question: Who controls the Tenderloin? Each time the question was asked, he'd drawn a blank. The men in the Barbary Coast saloons had scratched their heads and appeared stumped. So far as they knew, the Tenderloin had no boss. Something of a neutral zone, it seemed to run itself. The police kept it cordoned off for the gentry, and the lowlifes avoided it on threat of a billy club upside the head and a night in jail. The playground of the rich, it was thought to be immune to the overtures of crime bosses and vice lords.

Starbuck thought otherwise. A suspicion began to form sometime that afternoon. Vague at first, it slowly blossomed, and by the time he walked from the fourth saloon, it had taken form. Despite all he'd heard, he believed there was most definitely a boss of the Tenderloin. Further, he thought it quite likely that the same man was the underworld czar of San Francisco. An overlord who dictated to both Denny O'Brien and Fung Jing Toy.

He'd seen it happen closer to home. For the past decade, a shadowy, unobtrusive man named Lou Blomger had ruled Denver from behind the scenes. It made sense that a similar situation existed in San Francisco, where the pickings were riper and vice even more prevalent. The temptation was simply too great. With the amount of money involved, someone who dealt in grand schemes would have built himself an underworld empire. That he stayed out of the limelight, operating in the dark, made it no less real. To Starbuck, it seemed undeniable, chiseled in stone. All he had to do was prove it.

However it turned out, everything he'd learned had merely reinforced his original thought. The place to start was Denny O'Brien. He even had a cover story in mind, and instinct told him the Barbary Coast boss would go for it bait and all. From there, it was simply a matter of allowing nature to take its course. Red Ned Adair had the balls, and Denny O'Brien called the shots, but they both danced to another man's tune. Time, and a bit of luck, would reveal his name.

That evening Starbuck caught the night train for Los Angeles.

The city of angels was somewhat provincial and backwoodsy compared to San Francisco. Yet, while it lacked a cosmopolitan flavor, Los Angeles was nonetheless prosperous. Certain shops in the downtown area catered to those with money to burn. However excessive the demand, a man willing to pay the price could indulge almost any whim. All within a matter of hours.

Starbuck went directly from the train station to a men's haberdashery. He knew little about Los Angeles itself, but he had developed contacts throughout the West. In his business, the tools of the trade were dictated by the nature of the case, and time was often a factor. From his contacts, he knew where to go and who to see, no matter how strange the request. While he could have satisfied the same needs in San Francisco, it might very well have compromised the case. Secrecy and a whole new identity were essential to his plan. He would depart Los Angeles a different man from the one who had arrived on the morning train. And no one in San Francisco the wiser.

At the haberdashery, Starbuck spoke privately with the proprietor. He indicated that money was no object, so long as the service met his demands. He wanted a complete wardrobe—expensive clothes with the look of hand-tailored garments—and he wanted it no later than four o'clock that afternoon. The proprietor, with a nose for profit, assured him the deadline was no problem.

A clerk materialized at Starbuck's elbow, and a tailor was summoned from the back room. Under the proprietor's watchful eye, an array of clothing was selected from the racks and paraded before Starbuck for his approval. He chose four single-breasted suits, all fashionably cut and dazzling in color, ranging from pearl-gray to lush chocolate. He next selected several brocaded vests, gaudy to the extreme and color-coordinated with the suits. Then he picked out ruffled linen shirts, cravats and string ties, and a half-dozen sets of silk underwear. A brown derby and a gray fedora, along with three pairs of kidskin boots, were added to the pile. His last purchase was a matched set of hand-rubbed leather luggage.

A meticulous fitting session followed. One at a time, Starbuck changed into the suits and stood before a full-length mirror. The tailor, his mouth stuffed full of pins, took a nip here and a tuck there. When he finished, the suit jackets and trousers draped perfectly, with the rich appearance of clothes crafted stitch by stitch. Once more in his old suit, Starbuck paid the bill and added an extra hundred for good measure. The proprietor, bowing profusely, escorted him to the door. His wardrobe would be packed and waiting at the appointed time.

On the street, Starbuck hailed a hansom cab and gave the driver the name of a local dentist. Pleased with his progress thus far, he rolled himself a smoke and settled back in the seat. He'd spent somewhat more time than intended at the haberdashery, and he quickly calculated the cash left in his money belt. He judged the amount—$3,000—adequate for what remained to be done. If not, then he would wire his bank in Denver and arrange a speedy transfer of funds. Bankers, very much like whores, would always accommodate their select clientele.

Starbuck worked at his profession by choice rather than need. He was a man of considerable means, with a portfolio of municipal bonds and commercial real estate valued in excess of $250,000 on the open market. Not quite two years ago, he had inherited the largest cattle spread in the Texas Panhandle. The owner of the ranch, who was his closest friend and something of a surrogate father, had no family and had therefore designated him sole heir. Forced to choose between ranching and the detective business, he'd found it to be no contest. He sold the ranch for $200,000 and worked out an arrangement whereby the bank would manage his holdings for a fixed fee. So far, he had no complaints. The bank had shown a respectable return on his investments, and the financial independence enabled him to accept only those cases that piqued his interest. His net worth was a matter he thought of only rarely. He considered manhunting a far more rewarding endeavor.

The dentist was a slender man, completely bald, with innocent brown eyes. After being ushered into his office, Starbuck explained precisely what he had in mind. He wanted a gold sleeve fitted over his right front tooth, and anchored securely. Once in place, he concluded, it must appear to be a genuine gold tooth.

"A fake tooth?" the dentist asked, as if he couldn't have heard correctly. "You want a fake *gold* tooth?"

"A fake tooth," Starbuck corrected, "that looks like the real article."

"Why?" the dentist said, bewildered. "To what purpose?"

Starbuck smiled. "Ask me no questions and I'll tell you no lies. Can you do it?"

"I suppose so"—the dentist shrugged, eyebrows raised—"assuming you're willing to pay the price."

"How much?"

"A hundred dollars, plus the cost of the gold."

"Done." Starbuck pulled out his wallet. "One more thing. It has to be ready by four this afternoon. "

"Impossible! I'll need at least a week."

Starbuck extracted three hundred-dollar bills from his wallet and spread them on the desk. "A day's work for a week's pay. Interested?"

The dentist pocketed the bills and pointed to a high-backed operating chair. "Have a seat. I'll have to take some measurements."

"You come highly recommended, Doc. Don't disappoint me."

"Recommended by whom?"

"Like I said, ask me no questions—"

"Very well, no more questions. Let's get on with it."

Starbuck moved to the chair and seated himself. The dentist selected several instruments from a cabinet, then pried Starbuck's mouth open and began taking measurements. Ten minutes later he walked from the office and flagged another hansom cab.

The next stop on Starbuck's itinerary was a posh jewelry store. His shopping list was itemized, though flexible, and the purchases required only a few minutes. He selected a diamond pinky ring, with a stone only slightly smaller than a sugar cube. Then he chose a garish horseshoe-shaped diamond stickpin, with matching cuff links. His last purchase was a diamond-studded pocketwatch the size of a teacup. When the lid was opened, it chimed a musical rendition of *"Darling Clementine."*

There was no haggling, and he again paid in bills of large denominations. He stuffed the new watch into his vest pocket and threaded the heavy gold chain through a buttonhole. The old watch, along with the other items, were casually dropped into his jacket pocket. The jeweler watched the whole procedure with an expression of bemused wonder. He was still clutching a fistful of hundred-dollar bills when Starbuck hurried out the door.

One last stop completed Starbuck's shopping spree. The store was located on a sidestreet, with a small wooden sign pegged to the wall. The gunsmith's name was John Bohannon, and his work was known to lawman and outlaw alike. He was a master craftsman of the concealed weapon.

The inside of the store looked like an ordnance depot. The walls were lined with pistols of every description, and a double-shelved showcase was filled with pocket derringers and cut-down revolvers. Bohannon rose from a workbench at the rear of the store and moved to the showcase. He was a short, rotund man, with a shock of white hair and metal-framed glasses that magnified his eyes like a telescope. He greeted Starbuck genially.

"Afternoon. What can I do for you today?"

"I need a couple of guns," Starbuck told him. "One belly-gun and one hideout, the smaller the better."

"What caliber?" Bohannon asked pleasantly. "I've got everything from twenty-two to forty-five."

Starbuck's mouth curled. "Large enough to stop a man when he's centered the first shot."

Bohannon's eyes gleamed behind the bottle-thick glasses. "I take it you're an experienced shootist?"

"I generally hit the mark."

"Then something in forty-one ought to do the trick."

Bohannon bent over the showcase and took out a Colt Lightning. Only recently introduced, the revolver was double-action and fired a .41-caliber slug. The barrel and ejector rod had been trimmed to three inches. For a hideout gun, he suggested the Colt New House Model. A stubby five-shot revolver, it was chambered for .38 caliber. The birdshead grip was framed with ivory handles, and the sheathed trigger was activated by cocking the hammer. The barrel length was one and a half inches, and the entire gun could be covered by a normal handspan.

Starbuck handled the guns, testing them for balance and smoothness of action. The workmanship was flawless, and he quickly approved both selections. Bohannon outfitted him with a shoulder holster for the Lightning, and a clip-on boot holster for the hideout gun.

A box of cartridges for each gun completed the deal, and Starbuck gladly forked over nearly two hundred dollars. They shook hands and parted, never once having exchanged names.

Outside, Starbuck checked his new timepiece. The watch chimed three and merrily trilled "Darling Clementine." He smiled and mentally reminded himself to wire Mattie Silks, a Denver madam who owed him a favor. Once the message was sent, all that remained was to collect his wardrobe and the gold tooth. His disguise was set and his cover story would bear scrutiny. The northbound train departed at six, and from there it was on to San Francisco and his next stop.

The Barbary Coast and Denny O'Brien.

Chapter Five

Starbuck arrived at the Palace Hotel late the next morning. A doorman approached, but he bounded down from the hansom cab without assistance. Slipping the man a five spot, he jerked his thumb at his luggage. Then he stepped back, craning his head upward, and ogled the architecture.

Considered San Francisco's finest, the hotel was a structure of Olympian proportions. The building occupied an entire city block, and construction costs were reported to have exceeded $5,000,000. The entranceway was an immense courtyard, surrounded by galleries lofting seven stories high. Overhead, a domed skylight flooded the courtyard with a brilliant rainbow of colors. Already a legend to world travelers, the Palace was a home-away-from-home for visiting royalty and other people of wealth.

With the doorman at his heels, Starbuck swept into the lobby. He was attired in a getup of spectacular vulgarity. He wore a pearl-gray suit, with a sapphire-blue cravat and a brocaded vest to match. Diamonds spar-

kled from his ring and cuff links and stickpin with taw-
dry opulence. A cigar was wedged in the corner of his
mouth, and his gold tooth gleamed like a lighthouse
beacon.

Halfway to the front desk he suddenly stopped. The
lobby floor was paved with silver dollars set in dark
marble, and he gazed down on the sight with a look of
pop-eyed wonder. The fashionably dressed men and
women strolling through the lobby meanwhile paused
and stared at him like a sideshow freak escaped from
a circus. An interval of absolute silence stretched to
several moments. Then, with a loud snort, he shook
his head.

"Jeeezus Christ! Flat knocks your eyes out!"

Puffing clouds of smoke, he munched his cigar and
proceeded across the lobby. He halted at the desk and
knuckled his fedora onto the back of his head at a
rakish angle. Grinning broadly, he nodded to the clerk.

"Harry Lovett's the name. I want the classiest suite
you've got."

The clerk peered down his nose. "Do you have a
reservation, sir?"

"Hell, no!" Starbuck trumpeted. "Harry Lovett don't
need no reservation. Now hop to it, sonny! Fix me up,
and none of your sass."

The clerk flushed and quickly produced a registration
card. Starbuck signed his alias with a bold stroke and
then dropped the pen on the desk. With obvious dis-
taste, the clerk picked up the card and studied it at
length.

"Have you stayed with us before, Mr. Lovett?"

"Nope," Starbuck said briskly. "This here's my first
trip to Frisco."

The clerk flinched. Only seamen and people of low
station referred to the city by the bay as "Frisco." By

his expression, it was apparent he had already relegated Harry Lovett to that category. He tapped the registration card on his fingertips.

"One moment, please."

Turning away, he walked to a door at the end of the desk. A small sign identified the room beyond as the manager's office. He knocked softly and entered. Starbuck rolled the cigar to the opposite side of his mouth and looked bored. Then he noticed a stack of brochures on the counter, emblazoned with the hotel's name. He took one off the top and made a show of moving his lips while he read.

The brochure, meant to delight and inform, was a compendium of statistical trivia. Built by William Ralston, one of the city's leading industrialists, the Palace was an eclectic blend of rococo Victorian and ornate Louis XV. The hotel could accommodate twelve hundred guests and there was a fireplace in every room. A total of twenty thousand silver dollars were inset into the lobby floor, and there were nine hundred cuspidors scattered throughout the hotel. A hallmark of service, there were four hundred thirty-nine bathrooms, which provided the luxury of one bathroom for every 2.7 guests. In keeping with the overall decor, the toilet seats were specially crafted of Chippendale, that most revered of British imports. The cost of the toilet seats alone exceeded—

Starbuck stopped reading. He thought to himself he really wasn't out of place at the Palace. He was acting the part of a coarse, loud-mouthed vulgarian. The hotel, bragging about its toilet seats, was somewhat in the same league. For all their pretensions, the rich crowd wasn't above flaunting their built-for-a-king crappers.

The office door opened and the room clerk bustled

forward. He stopped and carefully laid the card on the desk. His expression was dour.

"Mr. Lovett, the manager has asked me to inform you of hotel policy. A guest who hasn't stayed with us previously is required to pay at least two days in advance. As you can appreciate, our suites are commodious and therefore quite expensive. So if you would care to look elsewhere—"

"Sounds fair." Starbuck took out his wallet and fanned ten one-hundred dollars bills across the counter. "A thousand ought to do for openers. You tell me when that runs out and I'll pony up some more."

The clerk sighed and reluctantly scooped the bills into a cash drawer. Without a word, he walked to the letter boxes, fished out a room key, and returned to the desk. He snapped his fingers, signaling a bellboy.

"Bellman! Suite four-o-six for Mr. Lovett."

Starbuck started away, then turned back. "Say, almost forgot to ask. Which way's the Barbary Coast?"

The clerk looked aghast. "Simply walk in the direction of the waterfront, Mr. Lovett. I'm told it's difficult to miss."

"You mean to say you've never been there?"

"No." The clerk drew himself up stiffly. "Never."

"Damn shame," Starbuck said with a waggish grin. "You ought to turn loose and live a little. We only pass this way once, and that's a mortal fact."

Starbuck pulled out his diamond-studded watch and popped the lid. The strains of "Darling Clementine" tinkled across the lobby. Hotel guests standing nearby turned to stare and the clerk rolled his eyes toward the ceiling. Starbuck snapped the lid closed and replaced the watch in his vest pocket.

"How long does it take to walk there?"

"A matter of a few minutes, no more."

"Much obliged."

"All part of the service, Mr. Lovett."

Starbuck flipped him a salute and strode off toward the elevators. The bellboy hefted his luggage and hurried along behind. Watching them, the clerk passed his hand in front of his eyes, and slowly shook his head.

Shortly after one o'clock Starbuck pushed through the doors of the Bella Union. The noontime rush had slacked off, and there were perhaps a dozen men strung out along the bar. He hooked a heel over the brass rail and nodded pleasantly to the bartender.

"Your boss a fellow by the name of Denny O'Brien?"

"Six days a week and all day on Sunday."

"Where might I find him?"

The barkeep ducked his chin. "See that gent down there?"

Starbuck glanced toward the end of the bar. A man stood hunched over the counter, staring dully into a glass of whiskey. He was wide and tall, with brutish features and a barrel-shaped torso. His head was fixed directly upon his shoulders, and he appeared robust as an ox. Starbuck recognized him instantly as a bruiser. One of a breed, bouncers and strongarm men, who maintained order with sledgehammer fists.

"Yeah, so?" Starbuck asked. "What about him?"

"You want to see Mr. O'Brien, you start with him. His name's High Spade McQueen."

"Sounds like a gamblin' man."

The barkeep smiled. "If I was you, I wouldn't bet against him. You might try talking real polite, too."

"That tough, huh?"

"Mister, he's a cross between a buzz saw and a grizzly bear. You never seen anything like him."

"Thanks for the tip."

Starbuck shoved away from the bar and walked toward the rear of the room. He braced himself to appear bluff and hearty, a man of dazzling good humor. Working undercover, he always turned actor, assumed a role, and it wouldn't do to slip out of character. He rounded the end of the bar and halted. Smiling affably, he showed High Spade McQueen his gold tooth.

"Mr. McQueen?"

"Who're you?"

"Name's Harry Lovett," Starbuck replied. "I've come all the way from Denver to see Denny O'Brien. The barkeep told me to check with you."

McQueen swiveled his head just far enough to look around. An ugly scar disfigured one cheek and his eyes were like ball bearings. He fixed Starbuck with a sullen stare.

"You got business with Mr. O'Brien?"

"I bear greetings from a mutual friend, Mattie Silks. She was of the opinion Mr. O'Brien and me might do one another a favor."

"Such as what?"

"I'm here to buy some whores. I need advice, and I'm willing to pay handsomely to get it."

McQueen's mouth split in a grotesque smile. His teeth were yellow as a row of old dice, and the scar distorted his features. He pushed off the bar.

"You should've said so to start with. C'mon, I'll take you up to the office."

He crossed the room and mounted the staircase. Starbuck obediently tagged along. From the rear, he was even more aware of the man's massive shoulders. He reminded himself to strike the first punch if ever he locked horns with High Speed McQueen.

Upstairs, McQueen turned into a small alcove off the central hallway. There was a door at the end of the alcove, and the balcony afforded a commanding view of both the theater and the barroom. He rapped on the door and a muffled voice from inside responded. Entering, he waved Starbuck through the door.

Denny O'Brien was stooped over a steel floor safe. He shot McQueen a look of annoyance, then quickly closed the safe door and spun the combination knob. Before the door swung shut, Starbuck caught a glimpse of several ledgers and neatly stacked rows of cash. His expression betrayed nothing.

"Sorry, boss," McQueen apologized in a low rumble. "Thought you'd be done by now."

"You're not paid to think!" O'Brien said curtly. "What do you want?"

"This here feller's named Lovett. Says he come all the way from Denver to see you."

"Yessir, Harry Lovett." Starbuck moved forward, hand extended. "And let me say it's an honor to meet you, Mr. O'Brien! Heard lots about you, and all of it good."

O'Brien held out a square, stubby-fingered hand. He shook once, a hard up-and-down pump, then let go. He gave Starbuck's getup a swift appraisal, noting the diamonds and the dapper cut of the clothes.

"Who's been telling you all these good things?"

"Mattie Silks," Starbuck lied heartily. "She says there's only one man to grease the wheels in Frisco, and that man's your very own self."

"Did she, now?" O'Brien sounded flattered. "I haven't laid eyes on Mattie in four, maybe five, years."

"Well you made an impression on her, Mr. O'Brien. I'm here to tell you she tagged you for a real stemwinder."

"Have a seat."

O'Brien crossed behind the desk and lowered himself

into an overstuffed judge's chair. His churlish manner seemed to moderate. His ruddy features thawed slightly and his eyes were friendly but sharp. Very sharp.

Hat in hand, Starbuck took a chair directly before the desk. Once more he marked that O'Brien's whole being was charged with energy, alive and very shrewd. Up close, there was a strong sense of animal magnetism about the man. A sense of lightning intelligence and feral cunning, underscored by a sharp odor of danger. Starbuck was also aware that O'Brien's gorilla had taken a position by the door, immediately behind him. Apparently a stranger was to be trusted no further than arm's length.

O'Brien eyed him in silence for a moment. "You a friend of Mattie's?"

"Yessir, I am," Starbuck said stoutly. "Mattie and me go back a long ways."

"You're from Denver, then?"

"On again, off again." Starbuck flipped a palm back and forth. "I drift around, generally the mining camps. A man in my line's got to go where the action's the hottest."

"What line would that be, just exactly?"

"Confidence games. Leastways, it was. You might say I've retired from the profession."

"Oh?" O'Brien said lazily. "How so?"

Starbuck gave him a jolly wink. "Hooked myself the prize sucker of all time. Took him for a bundle and figured I'd make a clean break, put my flim-flam days behind me. So I decided to go legit."

"I get the feeling legit doesn't mean reformed."

"You bet your socks it don't!"

"You've got a new line in mind, is that it?"

"Yes, indeedee!" Starbuck said with great relish. "I

aim to open a string of cathouses like nothing nobody's ever seen. Corner the market, in a manner of speaking."

"Corner the market where?"

"The mining camps." Starbuck lit a cigar, puffing grandly. "Leadville, Cripple Creek, four or five of the bigger camps. I'll make an absolute goddamned fortune!"

"Yeah?" O'Brien looked skeptical. "Last I heard, there wasn't any shortage of whores in the mining camps."

Starbuck woofed a bellylaugh. "Mr. O'Brien, them miners are queer birds. They'll pay double for anything that speaks foreign or looks the least bit different. So I figure to give 'em a crack at something besides white women."

"Like what?"

"China whores."

"Wait a minute!" O'Brien said bluntly. "Are you saying Mattie sent you to see me about slant-eyes?"

"She sure did," Starbuck acknowledged. "I don't know my ass from a bass bassoon about Chinamen. Never dealt with one in my life. She thought maybe you'd act as a go-between for me."

"A middleman?"

"No, not exactly. I'll make my own deal, but I need someone to open the door. Way I hear it, them Chinamen won't traffic with just anybody when it comes to slave girls."

"You plan to buy them outright, then?"

"For a fact," Starbuck said with cheery vigor. "An even hundred."

"A hundred?" O'Brien repeated, suddenly dumbstruck. "You mean to buy *one hundred* slave girls?"

"I like round numbers. Course, I'm not after just any

girls." Starbuck paused, admired the tip of his cigar. "They've got to be virgins."

"Virgins!" O'Brien stared at him with a burlesque leer of disbelief. "You want a hundred *virgins?*"

Starbuck let the idea percolate a few moments. "All virgins—and the whole kit and caboodle ages twelve to sixteen."

A smile formed at the corner of O'Brien's mouth, then broke into laughter. "By God, you think big, don't you? A hundred little China dolls!" He threw back his head and roared. "With their cherries intact, for Chrissake!"

Starbuck gave him a foolish grin. "Well, don't you see, them miners will really go for little girl whores, specially the innocent kind. By kicking things off with Chinee heathen virgins, I'll put the other cathouses in the shade damn near overnight. After that, nobody'll be able to touch my operation."

"Hell, I believe you!" O'Brien shook his head with admiration. "But you're talking about a shit-pot full of money. A hundred virgins won't come cheap."

"No problem," Starbuck said equably. "I'm loaded and willing to pay plenty, just so long as I get what I want."

O'Brien eyed him craftily. "What about me? Here in Frisco, a go-between doesn't come cheap, either."

Starbuck ventured a smile. "How does five percent strike you?"

"It gets my attention." O'Brien shrugged noncommittally. "I'd listen a lot closer if you were to say ten percent."

"One of the last things Mattie told me was that you wouldn't try to stiff me. You open the right door and you've got yourself a deal."

There was a moment of weighing and deliberation.

O'Brien thought it the most outlandish idea he'd ever heard. Yet that very oddity gave it a certain credibility. Nobody but a dimwitted fool would invent such a weird and grandiose story. While Harry Lovett was a smooth talker, he was clearly no simpleton, and everything about him reeked of money. O'Brien hadn't the vaguest notion of the asking price for a hundred slave-girl virgins. Whatever the amount, it would be steep, approaching the six-figure mark. A piece of any action that sweet was too tempting to resist.

"You're on," he said at length. "I'll set up a meeting with the head Chink in Chinatown. His name's Fung Jing Toy."

Starbuck flashed his gold tooth in a nutcracker grin. He looked pleased as punch and it was no act. Today was only a first step, but his instinct hadn't played him false.

Denny O'Brien had swallowed the bait whole.

Chapter Six

Chinatown was a world apart.

Upon crossing the intersection of Dupont and Washington, the white man's domain abruptly ended. From there, as though transported backward in time, the outsider had a sense of having entered Old Cathay. An ancient culture, unchanged for thousands of years, made only surface concessions to the blue-eyed white devils. Underneath, the old ways still existed.

In the lowering dusk, Starbuck walked along Washington Street. His appointment with Fung Jing Toy was for seven o'clock. All afternoon messsages had passed back and forth between the Chinatown vice lord and Denny O'Brien. The working arrangement between them was apparently civil, but larded with distrust and an element of rivalry. Fung's initial response, relayed by High Spade McQueen, had expressed cautious interest. Then, as the negotiations progressed, further information had been requested with respect to Harry Lovett's background. Finally, with O'Brien's assurance that the slave girls were intended for Colorado brothels, the vice lord acceded. Late that afternoon, a time had been set for the meeting.

Starbuck, meanwhile, was pumping Denny O'Brien. He'd spent the afternoon with the Barbary Coast boss, still play-acting the glib and garrulous con man turned whoremaster. His questions were reasonable, and framed in a manner that made O'Brien his ally, something of a conspirator. To dicker successfully for the slave girls, he explained, he needed some general idea as to whom he was dealing with and what sort of reception he might expect. O'Brien, who evidenced no great charity toward Chinatown's vice lord, was only too happy to oblige. He spoke at length, and with considerable authority, on Fung's rise to power. What he had to say was revealing, and recounted with a certain grudging admiration. He described a man of obsessive ambition and savage methods.

Fung Jing Toy had immigrated to America at the age of five. As a child he witnessed the eary tong wars on the streets of Chinatown, supporting himself as an apprentice to a shoemaker. A quick learner, ever willing to bend the rules, he displayed a compulsive drive to get ahead. At twenty-one, cloaked by a lily-white front, he began manufacturing shoes under the name of J. C. Peters & Company. The firm, however, was merely a legitimate base for criminal intrigue. He soon expanded into fan-tan parlors, opium smuggling, and prostitution. All the while, his horizons continued to broaden.

Early in 1876, Fung seized power of the Sum Yop tong. His next move, an open challenge to the other tong leaders, seemed suicidal. His gang began highjacking shipments of slave girls and assorted contraband being smuggled into San Francisco by the opposing factions. With little regard for human life, he provoked the bloodiest street war in Chinatown's history. Over a period of four years, his *boo how doy* hatchet men butchered more than a hundred of their rivals. By 1880, the other tongs were whipped into submission. A truce conference was convened, and Fung emerged the absolute ruler of Chinatown.

Since then, he had consolidated his power with ruthless efficiency. Once a week, his henchmen collected a percentage of gross receipts from all vice enterprises. Those who welched, or attempted to hold out, were swiftly raided by the police. Or in extreme circumstances, they were murdered as an object lesson. All legitimate businesses, importers and merchants alike, were required to pay weekly tribute for protection. The alternative was an unexplained fire, or a midnight visit from a squad of hatchet men. The slavegirl trade, once an open market, was now Fung's province alone. Only those who obtained his sanction were allowed to traffic in human cargo.

A traditionalist, Fung still observed the old customs. He dressed like his forefathers, affected humility, and lived in a modest house on Washington Street. He was a student of art and ancient scrolls, and his own poetry was said to contain such subtle nuances that it could not be translated into English. A playwright as well, he wrote dramas which were performed at the Chinese Theater on Jackson Street. According to rumor, he subsidized the theater and was a patron to those who displayed artistic merit.

Yet, for all his benevolent mannerisms, he had the killer instinct of a cobra and a barbaric sense of survival. Assassination by other tong leaders was an ever-present danger, and his personal living quarters were virtually impregnable. The barred steel door, leading into a suite of rooms without windows, was guarded by a pair of Tibetian mastiffs. At all times, night and day, he was also accompanied by two *boo how doy* hatchet men. Not surprisingly, his death was widely contemplated but rarely attempted.

Starbuck was intrigued by the man. From all he'd been told, Fung was an enigma, the inscrutable Oriental of legend. A vicious killer who wrote poetry and performed masterfully on the zither. A philanthropist who traded in slave girls and extorted tribute from his own countrymen. A throwback to the warlords of old, at once civilized and savage. In short, a man of many parts, and worth meeting.

Chinatown itself seemed no less a paradox. Walking along Washington, Starbuck thought to himself that it was actually a city within a city. One big tenement, it was dirty and overcrowded, squalid and diseased. The people lived in cellars and back-alley rabbit warrens, musty wooden cubicles. The women were dressed in black pantaloons and long smocks, and the men, their hair braided in pigtails, wore floppy jackets and baggy pajama pants. Most spoke only the dialect of their native land, and those who could converse with a Westerner resorted to pidgin English that was all but incomprehensible. A stranger asking directions might as well have talked to a deaf mute.

Washington Street, otherwise known as the Street of the Thousand Lanterns, teemed with people. The sweet smell of opium and the stench of sweaty bodies intermingled in an oppressive odor. The shops and stores, displaying their wares, added to the rank aroma. Dried sea horses and pickled squid were heaped in a herbalist's window. A grocer's storefront exhibited row upon row of plucked chickens and skinned ducks, dangling from overhead beams. Sidewalk bins overflowed with winter melons and rotting vegetables, and a fish peddler operated from an open cart on the corner. Amid the din of commerce, there was human barter, as well.

Crib whores, imprisoned behind barred windows, talked up their trade. The lowest form of slave girls, they wore only short blouses, naked from the waist down. Chinese men were addressed in the native tongue, and offered unknown splendors at reduced rates. White men, thought to be ignorant and lavish spenders, brought on a frantic singsong chant.

"Chinee girl velly nice! Looksee tow bits, feelee floor bits. Doee only six bits!"

Hurrying past, Starbuck was reminded that the plumbing of Oriental women was thought to be different from that of white women. To the uninitiated, it was commonly believed that their private parts went east-west instead of north-south. The debate, actively fostered by the Chinese, had produced a thriving, if somewhat bizarre, sideline to the oldest profession. A curious customer could have a looksee for two bits, a mere twenty-five cents. Or if he cared to check out the plumbing personally, he could have a feelee for four bits. That served to settle the east-west question, and often led to an additional sale. For another quarter, a total of six bits, he could actually doee. Quick as a wink, for the crib girls were also velly fast, all doubt was then removed.

Starbuck was something of a novice himself. He'd talked countless girls, from schoolmarms to saloon tarts, out of their drawers and into bed. Yet he had never been in the sack with an Oriental woman. He knew the east-west question was sheer tomfoolery, but he thought it might be worth a try while he was in Frisco. Whichever direction the plumbing ran, it would be worth the price of admission. A little doee now and then kept a man from going stale.

A couple of minutes before seven, Starbuck located Fung's house. As he'd been told, it was the only three-story building in all of Chinatown that wasn't swarming with a hundred or more occupants. He rapped on the door and almost instantly it swung open. A servant bowed him inside, quickly closing and bolting the door. Without a word, the man turned and walked along a central hallway.

Starbuck followed. He checked left and right, naturally curious about the inside of a Chinese home. Yet there was little to see; the rooms off the corridor were dark; except for dim candles and several large vases, the hall itself was bare. He had the sense of being watched, which was reinforced by the servant's casual manner. He wondered how many hatchet men silently waited in the darkened rooms.

At the end of the hallway, the servant stopped and bowed him through a door. Stepping onto a small landing, Starbuck saw a lighted staircase leading to the cellar. He went down the stairs, which turned sharply at the bottom, and emerged in an underground chamber. One look and he understood immediately why Chinatown's vice lord still survived.

The chamber ran the width of the house. Ornate candle fixtures were attached to the walls, and a steel door stood opposite the staircase. Before the door, chained to the wall, were two beasts that vaguely resembled dogs. Huge as tigers, the mastiffs looked as though they would happily devour a man for breakfast. The dogs snarled in unison, and showed him fangs the size of tusks. He remained very still.

A Chinaman appeared in the doorway. At his command, the mastiffs dropped to the floor, silent but watchful. Another man came through the door and paused, hands stuffed up his sleeves. Tall men, muscular and hard-faced, they both wore broad-brimmed flat hats, their hair twisted in long queues. Their robes were black and their rubber-soled shoes made every movement silent as a whisper. From the look of them, there was a hatchet up every sleeve.

Starbuck thought he'd never seen men who so thoroughly fitted the part of assassins. The first one expertly patted him down, and removed the Colt Lightning from his shoulder holster. The hideout gun in his boot top went undetected, and knowing it was there gave him some degree of comfort. Still, even though he was armed, he warned himself to play it fast and loose. A bold front and quick wits were the key to leaving the chamber alive.

The hatchet man in the doorway moved aside and motioned him through. Starbuck gingerly stepped past the mastiffs and entered a spacious room. Spartan as a monk's cell, the room was furnished with floor cushions and a low teakwood table. To his immediate left was another steel door, which he assumed led to the living quarters. The hatchet men took up positions directly behind him, one on either side of the entranceway. He needed no reminder that it was also the only way out.

The side door opened and Fung Jing Toy whisked into the room. He wore a silk mandarin gown and a black skullcap. A slender man, with a long mustache and skin the texture of parchment, his bearing was that of someone who spends his life remote from the world of people. His eyes were impersonal.

"Mr. Lovett." His head dipped in a bow. "Please be seated."

"Thank you kindly."

Starbuck lowered himself onto one of the cushions. His legs were too long to fit under the table, and he awkwardly twisted around sideways. Fung moved to the opposite side of the table and took a seat, legs crossed. A moment passed; then he nodded with grave courtesy and spoke in a reedy voice.

"I am told this is your first visit to our city."

"That's a fact. Got in late this morning."

"Have your expectations been fulfilled?"

"Well . . ." Starbuck smiled lamely. "I've been pretty busy. Haven't had much time to catch the sights."

"A situation not without remedy. You must allow us to show you something of Little China during your stay."

"Little China?"

"A colloquial expression," Fung said with a patronizing smile. "Your people call it Chinatown. We find our own name more suitable."

Starbuck realized the vice lord's smile was closer to a grimace. A cold rictus that touched his lips but never his eyes. The serpentine charm and oily manner also failed to hide the hauteur in his voice, the deep arrogance. Still, there was no faulting the man's command of English. He spoke with only a slight accent, and he used three-dollar words. Starbuck thought "colloquial" was a real piss-cutter. He made a mental note to look it up in the dictionary.

"Now, as to business," Fung went on blandly. "Denny O'Brien informs me that you are interested in a purchase of some magnitude."

"All depends," Starbuck said tentatively. "The merchandise would have to be prime stuff, pick of the litter."

"Ah, yes." Fung permitted himself an ironic glance. "Pick of the litter meaning virgin girls, is it not so?"

"Nothing less," Starbuck affirmed. "Virgins will be the come-on, if you get my drift. I'll use 'em to start the operation off in real style."

Fung gave him a thoughtful stare. "I believe you plan to open several houses, all at the same time. To one of humble aspirations, that seems a grand and daring concept."

Starbuck beamed like a trained bear. "I think big and I'm willing to put my money where my mouth is. Four or five houses—all stocked with virgins—it'll flat knock their eyes out! No way it'll fail, and there's the God's own truth."

Fung studied his nails. "An ancient proverb advises us that truth wears many faces." He suddenly looked up, eyes gleaming icons. "I understand you are a man of some influence in the Colorado mining camps?"

"Well, let's just say I've got pull with all the right people."

"Then you must know my associate, Wong Sing? He resides in the town called Leadville."

"No." Starbuck sensed danger. "Never made his acquaintance."

"How is that possible?" Fung's eyes were now veiled. "He leads the Sum Yop tong in Leadville."

"What's his front?" Starbuck asked evenly. "What's he do for a living?"

"I am told he operates a laundry."

Starbuck opened his hands, shrugged. "Not too likely we would've met. See, I don't care much for starch in my shirts." He paused, flashed his gold tooth in a crafty smile. "I generally find a woman willing to do my wash."

The statement was entirely plausible. In mining camps, white men were fond of saying all Chinamen looked alike. Moreover, those Chinese who owned businesses invariably ran a laundry or back-alley café. So it was understandable that the one who called himself Harry Lovett would have no knowledge of Wong

71

Sing. Yet Fung was not wholly satisfied with the answer. He survived by trusting no man, most especially a blue-eyed devil endorsed by Denny O'Brien. He concluded the matter would bear further scrutiny.

A smile appeared at the corner of his mouth. "Upon your return, you must make yourself known to Wong Sing. He would be honored to be of service . . . should the occasion arise."

"I'll do that very thing," Starbuck said earnestly. "Who knows? Maybe we'll be able to swap favors here and there."

Fung laced his fingers together, considered a moment. "Your request is most unusual. A hundred virgins, all of such tender age, are not easily obtainable."

"No, I suppose not." Starbuck feigned a sly look. "Course, if I made it worth your while, you likely wouldn't have any trouble, would you?"

Fung nodded wisely. "I believe it could be arranged."

"How much?"

"One thousand dollars a girl."

"Holy Christ!" Starbuck appeared shocked. "That's a little steep, isn't it?"

"Perhaps," Fung intoned. "On the other hand, where else would you turn? I alone govern the trade in slave-girls."

"You've got a point." Starbuck hesitated, his features screwed up in a frown. "How would I know they're all virgins?"

"You have my word," Fung said in a voice without tone. "Or if you wish, you may have them inspected by a doctor. Such matters are readily arranged."

Starbuck pondered a moment, then laughed. "What the hell, it's only money! When can you make delivery?"

"Hmm." Fung nodded to himself as though possessed of some secret knowledge. "I will consult with my associates and advise you. These affairs must be conducted with a certain delicacy."

Starbuck found the statement too cryptic for comfort. "Don't hang me up too long. I'm already short on time."

"I beg your indulgence," Fung said politely. "In the meantime, allow us to entertain you. The treasures of Little China are many and varied . . . and quite often memorable."

Fung rose to his feet. Starbuck was assured he would be contacted, and on that note, the meeting ended. Bows were exchanged, then one of the hatchet men escorted Starbuck past the dogs and up the stairs. Once they were out of sight, Fung turned to the other guard with a look of sharp concern.

"Find May Ling!" he ordered. "Bring her to me now."

Chapter Seven

Starbuck had no illusions about the girl. She was a gift from Fung, a young seductress meant to please and delight him. Yet she was also a spy, an enchanting interrogator with both the beauty and the thorns of a rose. He had no doubt his every word was reported directly to her master.

The invitation was extended the morning after his meeting with Fung. At first, aware of the danger, his reaction was to politely decline. Denny O'Brien had already offered him one of the Bella Union girls, and that was excuse enough to beg off. Then, wary of insulting Fung, he thought it wiser to accept. There were grave risks entailed, but he was an old hand at guarding himself in the clinches. Besides, he was horny as a billygoat and still extremely curious about Chinese women. Until he verified it for himself, the question of their east-west plumbing would always stick in his mind. He accepted, and the engagement was arranged for that evening.

Shortly after sundown, one of Fung's men met him

outside the hotel. He was led to a building in the heart of Chinatown, then upstairs to an apartment on the second floor. The man knocked three times, bowed from the waist, and disappeared down the stairs. He was left alone before the door.

Whatever he expected, Starbuck was not prepared for the girl's loveliness. May Ling was tiny, with a doll-like figure and large almond-shaped eyes. Her features were exquisite, with bee-stung lips and high cheekbones, all framed by a mass of hair black as obsidian. Her voice was odd and vibrant, and there was about her an aura of innocence destroyed. She smelled sweet and alluring, and gave off a sensual radiation as palpable as musk. He judged her age at somewhere between eighteen and twenty. A child-woman of evocative beauty.

Her apartment was small but richly furnished. The walls were decorated with silk prints and the floors were lushly carpeted; the bureau and several squat chests were finished in black, heavily lacquered, and trimmed with brass fittings. A tall Oriental screen separated the living area from the bedchamber, and a miniature kitchen was partitioned off by yet another screen. A low table, used for both entertaining and dining, was surrounded by plush floor cushions.

May Ling was dressed in a milk-white kimono that seemed to mold her body in melted ivory. Her English, like Fung's, was remarkably correct, with only a trace of an accent. She greeted Starbuck with a cordial bow, and showed him to the place of honor at the table. In deference to his Western tastes, she served whiskey and provided a porcelain ashtray for his cigar. She was gracious, drawing him out with small talk, and gave no hint of embarrassment at the arrangement. She was there for his pleasure, and quite clearly eager to please.

Starbuck was indeed pleased. She was a creature of

surpassing beauty, and the atmosphere was conducive to thoughts of erotic Oriental mysteries. The scent of joss sticks and sandalwood was heady, somehow intoxicating, adding to the sensation of her nearness. When she spoke her lips moved like moth wings, and she seemed to have an infinite variety of smiles, all suggestive of the night ahead. He watched, sipping whiskey, while she glided spectrally from the kitchen to the table. His hunger, mounting steadily, was not for food.

Dinner was one surprise after another. She served prawns simmered in a sticky, sweet sauce, and something that vaguely resembled pork, swimming in a thick black gumbo. Steaming bowls of vegetables, similar in appearance to seaweed, complimented the meat dishes, and with each course there appeared another mound of snow-white rice. Herbal tea and delicate cookies, tasting faintly of ginger, finished off the meal.

Starbuck thoroughly stuffed himself. He'd never tasted prawns, and the other dishes, though equally unfamiliar, were nonetheless savory. After dinner, he loosened his belt a notch and lit a cigar. May Ling cleared the table and poured him another whiskey. Then she took a zither from a wall peg and seated herself across from him. Her fingers flew over the instrument like darting birds, producing a strange and haunting music. The sound was discordant to his ear, not unpleasant but seemingly without melody. To his amazement, she opened her mouth and began to sing. The words were meaningless, but the timbre of her voice was almost hypnotic, curiously intimate. Her gaze never left him, and he felt certain the song was meant to convey some seductive message. When she finished, he stuck the cigar in his mouth and applauded heartily. She blushed and modestly averted her eyes.

The evening thus far was beyond anything he had

imagined. The lavish meal and the haunting song were unaccustomed preliminaries to the mating ritual he normally practiced. Yet the girl herself was by far the greatest surprise. She had asked no questions and made no reference whatever to his dealings with Fung. Nor had she displayed even passing interest in who he was or where he came from, or the nature of his business. In short, she'd made no attempt to grill him, and seemed content merely with his company. He found himself somewhat bewildered, and more than a little curious. Tactfully, choosing his words, he asked her about herself. His interest was genuine, and from the expression in her eyes, he knew it was a question she'd seldom been asked. He prompted her, gently insistent, and she slowly began to talk.

Her life, she told him simply, had been ordained by circumstance. Her parents were poor, struggling to eke out an existence. Like many peasant girls, governed by a centuries old custom, she had been sold into bondage. The contract took effect on her tenth birthday, and by then she'd shown promise of beauty. One of Fung's agents ultimately bought her, and she had arrived in San Francisco not quite a year later. Unlike ordinary slave girls, Fung had taken a special interest in her. A tutor had been retained to teach her English and the art of conversation, and still another mentor had trained her in music and song. A woman of great wisdom had instructed her in lovemaking and the many exotic acts pleasurable to man. At age fourteen she had been accorded a great honor. Fung, her master and patron, had himself taken her virginity.

With a note of pride, she observed that since that time she had lived the life of a courtesan. She entertained those men, both Chinese and American, who were of special interest to her master. In return, she had been given her own quarters and the freedom to travel Little China as she pleased. Over the years many wealthy men had attempted to buy her, offering thousands of dollars above the price normally paid for even the most beautiful virgin. Yet, declaring her beyond value, her master had refused in each instance. That refusal had bestowed great honor on her, and wherever she went the people of Little China treated her with the respect reserved for one of position and rank. Few slave girls rose so high, and she considered herself the most fortunate of women. Not yet twenty, she had found serenity and purpose in life. She existed to serve her master, and her days were filled with happiness. She was content.

Starbuck believed her. She was a slave, and whether she called herself courtesan or whore, she would live out her days in bondage. All the same, she was happier than any white whore he'd ever known. She was at peace with herself and her world, and the serenity she spoke of was no act. Her voice, the expression in her eyes, told the story. She had found something in life that few people attain. Her mirror reflected the worth of her own esteem.

May Ling smiled and sang him another song. He lay back on the pillows, sipping whiskey and puffing his cigar. After a time, she put the zither away and held out her hand. He climbed to his feet, all but bewitched by her loveliness, and allowed himself to be led to her bedchamber. There she undressed him, and after stepping out of her kimono, she let him gaze a moment upon the golden swell of her breasts.

Then she showed him that Chinese girls were, after all, no different from white women. Some were simply better than others, and she skillfully persuaded him that she was the best.

May Ling never questioned her master's orders, or his motives. To her, a man's body was like a zither, an instrument to be strummed and caressed. Several times during the night, using her own body to strike responsive chords, she had taught Starbuck exquisite harmonies known only to a trained courtesan. Early the next morning, she undertook the balance of her assignment.

After a late breakfast, she suggested a personally conducted tour of Little China. Starbuck was feeling a bit frazzled, his juices sapped by her arduous and sometimes gymnastic lovemaking. Under normal circumstances he might have hesitated, but his brain was muzzy and he suspected nothing. Chinatown was Fung's domain, and seeing it through May Ling's eyes seemed very much in order. He immediately approved the idea.

On the street, she took his arm and guided him toward the center of Little China. As they walked, she chattered on gaily, explaining that the district was the largest Chinese settlement outside the Orient. Within a dozen square blocks, some thirty thousand people lived and worked, rarely ever setting foot in the white sections of San Francisco.

The Chinese, May Ling noted proudly, were an industrious people. Some twisted cigars for a living, others worked in clothing and shoe factories, and many served in white homes as cooks and houseboys. For the most part, they were frugal, followed the ancient religious rites, and kept very much to themselves. Yet they were not the simple peasants, ignorant and humble, so commonly portrayed by whites. Almost all were fanatic gamblers, playing the lottery and fan-tan, and even a variation of poker. Opium smoking was widely practiced, and the trade in *gow* pills, pipe-size balls of opium, had evolved into a thriving industry. There were even exclusive establishments for white gentlemen and their ladies. Unlike common opium dens, the service there was discreet and costly, the *gow* pills of superb quality.

Still another misconception, May Ling went on, was the belief by whites that Orientals were sexually backward. To the contrary, the Chinese were a very sensual people, connoisseurs of the flesh. A Chinese man seldom limited himself to one woman, even if he was married and had a family. Nor was it considered shameful for a Chinese woman to enjoy the act, and express that joy through inventive byplay passed down from mother to daughter. In fact, the Oriental preoccupation with sex manifested itself in many forms. The most widely known was the flourishing trade in slave girls. Nowhere else on earth was the appreciation of eroticism so vividly demonstrated.

May Ling suddenly stopped. Her eyes seemed to sparkle with secret amusement. "Would you care to attend a slave-girl auction?"

"Would I!" Starbuck said, astonished. "I'd like nothing better."

"I believe one is being held this morning."

"You really think they'd let us watch? I've heard these things are sort of private, invitation only."

"Oh, yes," May Ling trilled happily. "You are with me, which means you are a very special friend of the master. We would not be turned away."

"Well, what are we waiting for? Hot damn, a real live slave-girl auction! You're just a sackful of surprises."

"Perhaps we shouldn't." May Ling mocked him with a tiny smile. "These girls are not virgins, and much older than those you wish to purchase. You might be disappointed."

Starbuck laughed. "Don't worry your pretty head about that. C'mon, chop, chop! Let's go!"

With a minxish giggle, May Ling took his arm and led him to the corner. There they turned onto a side-street, then walked toward a warehouse halfway down the block. A squad of hatchet men, uniformed in the regulation pajama suits and black hats, stood guard outside. Approaching them, May Ling let go a volley of Chinese, her tone gracious, yet somehow imperious. The men bowed respectfully, and one of them rushed to open the door. She stepped through, followed closely by Starbuck, and directed him to a vantage point along the wall. From there, they had an unobstructed view of the entire warehouse.

Starbuck was reminded of a livestock auction. A large crowd of men, both Chinese and white, were ganged around a wooden platform. The auctioneer, a jolly-eyed Chinaman with a loud mouth and a winning smile, walked the platform like a captain commanding the bridge of a ship. Beyond the platform, huddled together in a forlorn group, were a hundred or more Chinese girls. One at a time, they were brought forward by the auctioneer's assistants and stripped naked. Shoved onto the platform, they were then forced to parade before the crowd like prize broodmares. The prospective buyers were allowed to examine each girl before the bidding began.

May Ling briefly explained the complex system underlying the slave-girl trade. Her master placed an order with procurers in China for delivery in San Francisco on a certain date. Upon arrival, the girls were secreted in padded crates, invoiced as dishware, and American customs agents were bribed to pass the bales without inspection. While special orders were often filled for wealthy whites and prosperous Chinese tradesmen, the cargo was generally sold at open auction. The choicest girls, selected for their youth and attractiveness, were auctioned off to men looking for a concubine and jobbers who resold to smaller, inland markets. Prices varied from girl to girl, but usually started with a minimum bid of $200 and climbed to $500 or higher. The refuse, those unsuitable for auction, were sold to waterfront brothelkeepers or put to work in the Chinatown cribs.

The virgin market, May Ling remarked, was conducted on a somewhat higher level. Procurers in China contracted for the girls at an early age, generally two through five. The parents then raised the girls, and the procurer meanwhile contracted to deliver virgins of a specified age group, and on a specified date, in San Francisco. Even now, her master held contracts on some four hundred virgins, ages two through sixteen, who were available for delivery on demand. Thus, there was always a plentiful stock to supply future markets.

Starbuck listened with only one ear. His attention was fixed on the platform. Several men had stepped forward to probe and fondle a girl who looked to be no more than fourteen. She stood dull-eyed and submissive, abject in her nakedness. The auctioneer began the bidding at $200, and within minutes she was sold for $375. The man who bought her paid the auctioneer, and a bill of sale, with the girl's mark, was quickly produced. The document was legal and binding in American courts. There were quotas restricting Chinese immigration, but there were no laws forbidding the sale of Chinese girls into bondage. The young girl, now a legally bound slave, was swiftly dressed and hustled away by her new master.

"A fortunate girl," May Ling observed, noting his interest. "Had she not attracted a buyer, she might have joined those who work in the cribs."

"So young?" Starbuck said without thinking. "A girl that age in the cribs?"

"Oh, yes," May Ling replied, studying him with a half-smile. "But she would be much older tomorrow. The cribs age a girl quickly."

"How long do they last?"

"Four years, perhaps less," May Ling said in a low voice. "The work is hard, and men use them in cruel ways. Their minds go wrong, or they become diseased, and then they are no longer of value to their master."

Starbuck felt a sudden revulsion. "You mean they go crazy?"

"Some do." May Ling kept her tone casual. "For most, it is the sailor's disease—the pox—that claims them."

"What happens then?"

"They are sent to the hospital."

"Hospital?" Starbuck said, looking at her. "To be cured?"

"No, to die." Her appraisal of him was deliberate, oddly watchful. "The crib masters have a secret place they call the hospital. When a girl outlives her usefulness, she is taken there and given a pallet. An attendant places beside her a cup of water and a cup of rice, and a small oil lamp. He informs her that she must die by the time the oil burns out. Later, when he returns, the girl is almost always dead—sometimes by starvation, usually by her own hand."

"Jesus Christ!" Starbuck scowled, shook his head. "Some hospital."

"Yes." An indirection came into May Ling's eyes.

"The people of Little China call it 'the place of no return.'"

Too late, Starbuck sensed the trap. He wiped away the frown and quickly plastered a dopey smile across his face. Yet he wasn't at all sure he'd fooled May Ling. She'd brought him here, and purposely suckered him into a conversation about crib girls, all to get a reaction. That much was now abundantly clear, and he realized she was swifter than she appeared. No questions, no need to interrogate him. A night's lovemaking, and her innocent manner had effectively lowered his guard. Then she laid the bait and waited to see his reaction. A goddamned Oriental mousetrap! And he'd gone for the cheese.

"Well, now!" He gave her a lopsided grin. "Let's hope none of my little virgins ever needs a trip to the hospital."

"Would that bother you?"

"At a thousand bucks a head!" he roared. "You bet your sweet ass that'd bother me!"

She giggled softly. "Do you truly find it sweet?"

"Sweeter than sugar, and twice as nice!"

May Ling took his arm and they turned to leave the warehouse. On the street, Starbuck gave her a squeeze and made himself a promise. One more dip of the wick, then he'd ditch her fast.

And get the hell out of Chinatown.

Chapter Eight

The miners came in forty-nine
The whores in fifty-one.
And when they got together
They produced the Native Son.

Nell Kimball scarcely heard the lyrics. She was seated in a curtained loge with Starbuck, whose attention was directed to the stage. Covertly, out of the corner of her eye, she was watching him with a bemused look. She thought him a most unlikely whoremaster.

Onstage, a buxom songbird was belting out the tune in a loud, brassy voice. A ballad of sorts, it traced the ancestry of Nob Hill swells to the mating of whores and miners who had settled San Francisco during the Gold Rush. There was an element of truth to the ditty, and it was a favorite with audiences on the Barbary Coast. Tonight, the crowd in the Bella Union was clapping and stamping their feet, and roaring approval as the lyrics became progressively vulgar.

Starbuck looked like a peacock in full plumage. He was tricked out in diamonds and a powder-blue suit, with a paisley four-in-hand tie and a gaudy lavender shirt. The getup fitted the image of a whoremonger with grand ideas, but Nell Kimball was having second thoughts. Even the gold tooth left her unconvinced. Her whore's intuition told her Harry Lovett was something more than he appeared.

Earlier, Denny O'Brien had ordered her to entertain him royally. At first, she'd been a bit miffed, her vanity wounded. Harry Hovett had spent the last two days in Chinatown—doubtless getting himself screwed silly by Fung's prized hussy—and that put her in the position of playing second fiddle. Around the Bella Union she got top billing, acting as O'Brien's strong right arm. She supervised all the show girls, occasionally wooing a high roller personally, and she wasn't accustomed to standing in line behind a sloe-eyed Chinese slut. Yet orders were orders, and she'd learned the hard way never to provoke O'Brien's temper. He considered Lovett top-drawer business, and it wouldn't do to let Fung outshine them in the entertainment department. However she managed it, Lovett was to be given ace-high treatment, and made to forget the China girl's bedroom artistry. All of which meant a long night in the saddle.

For Starbuck's part, he felt like he'd come home. Nell Kimball was his kind of woman. Unlike May Ling's charade, there was no pretense about Nell, nothing phony. She was a saloon girl who had fought and clawed her way to the top of her profession. A tough cookie, honed by experience, she could handle a wise-ass chump or a mean-eyed drunk with equal ease. She looked to her own interests, always a step ahead of the competition, and God pity anybody who got in her way. Her counterpart was found in mining camps and cowtowns throughout the West, and she was the only kind of woman Starbuck fully understood. Moreover, he admired her for perhaps the best of reasons. Except that she wore bloomers, there wasn't a nickel's worth of difference between them. In all the things that counted, they were very much birds of a feather. Hard-headed realists, blooded but never whipped, survivors.

Then, too, Starbuck had to admit she was nothing shy in the looks department. She was compellingly attractive, tall and statuesque, with enormous hazel eyes and sumptuous figure. Her tawny hair was piled in coils and puffs atop her head, and she carried herself with assured poise. Her gaze was direct, filled with a certain bawdy wisdom, and she seemed to view the world with good-humored irony. He thought that was perhaps the one essential difference between them. He saw the world through the eyes of a confirmed cynic. She saw it through a prism that was still slightly rose-tinted, and he considered that a weakness.

By and by, perhaps later tonight, he fully intended to exploit that weakness. His visit to the slave-girl auction that morning, coupled with May Ling's boast-ful remarks about Fung, had merely strengthened his original assessment. Without an overlord to keep the peace, Chinatown and the Barbary Coast could not coexist. Denny O'Brien, given the scope of his ambi-tion, could never resist a takeover attempt in China-town. Someone restrained him from doing so, and that someone was the man who cracked the whip in San Francisco. Unless he missed his guess, Starbuck thought it entirely likely that Nell Kimball knew the someone's name. A gentle touch, and his softsoap routine, might very well persuade her to talk. Contrary to what peo-ple thought, the way to a whore's heart was not between her legs. Affection and kindness were what turned the trick.

The chesty songbird ended her number and the curtain rang down to wild applause. Starbuck poured champagne and lifted his glass in a toast. The evening was far along, but he'd made no overtures, no suggestive remarks. He figured it was a new experience for Nell, and certain to pique her interest. He wasn't far short of the mark.

"So tell me," she said with a quizzical look. "Have yourself a good time in Chinktown, did you?"

"No complaints," Starbuck allowed. "Course, I'd have to say those Chinamen take a little getting used to."

"Yeah, that Fung's a real pistol, isn't he?"

"I suppose he's all right . . . for a Chinaman."

"On the Coast, we call him Fung Long Dong."

"Oh?" Starbuck saw a glint in her eye. "Why's that?"

"Because he's got a permanent hard-on." Nell laughed at her racy admission. "Screws anything that's not nailed down. Women, girls, even little boys, so I've heard."

Her laugh was infectious, and Starbuck grinned. "Wouldn't surprise me. After seeing that three-ring circus he runs—the dogs and his hatchet men—I'd believe anything."

"Forget the dogs, honeybun! You just stay clear of Wong Yee and Sing Dock."

"His hatchet men?" Starbuck asked. "What's the story on them?"

"All bad," Nell said quietly. "When they kill someone, they tidy up the corpse's clothes, comb his hair, and press a smile on his mouth. God knows what they do before they kill him. They're both as queer as a three-dollar bill."

"No accounting for taste," Starbuck said with a crooked smile. "I've always preferred the ladies, myself."

Nell gave him a cool look. "How'd you like May Ling? Not that anybody ever called the little tramp a lady."

Starbuck mugged, hands outstretched. "A gentleman never tells. You're right about one thing, though—she's no lady!"

Nell warmed to the remark. "Well, it just bears out what I've always said. Those China girls have got no class. You're lots better off here on the Coast."

"Now that you mention it," Starbuck said casually, "I got pretty much the same story in Chinatown. The way Fung talks, there's no love lost between him and Denny."

"I guess not!" Nell tossed her head. "Denny would cut that Chink's heart out and dance on his grave."

"What stops him?"

"I don't follow you."

"What stops him from walking in there and taking over Chinatown? Hell, Fung and his hatchet men wouldn't stand a chance! If I was Denny, I'd do it in a minute."

Nell blinked and looked away. "You'd have to ask Denny about that. I keep my nose where it belongs."

"I'll bet!" Starbuck ribbed her. "Strikes me, you pretty much know what's going on around the Bella Union."

"Maybe I do," Nell observed neutrally. "But smart girls learn not to talk out of school, and I sit right up at the head of the class."

Starbuck let it drop for the moment. "Well, you're the number-one girl around here. No question about that! Wish to hell I had someone like you to run my operation. It'd sure take a load off my mind."

"Since you brought it up," Nell said slowly, "I'm curious about something. Have you ever operated a whorehouse before?"

"Nope." Starbuck's mouth widened in a devil-may-care grin. "But I'm all set to give 'er one helluva try!"

"You've got brass." Nell cocked her head in a funny little smile. "A hundred virgins and four whorehouses! How in God's name do you figure to pull it off?"

"I pray a lot," Starbuck said, deadpan. "Course, I've got a way with the ladies. So that ought to smooth things considerable."

"Now you're bragging."

"Think so?" Starbuck gave her a roughish wink. "There's one way to find out."

Nell laughed a low, throaty laugh. "Sounds like you're getting fresh, Mr. Lovett."

"The idea crossed my mind."

"Then I suppose we'll have to find out . . . won't we?"

Starbuck put his arm around her, and she scooted closer on the divan. The curtain rose and a line of can-can dancers went prancing across the stage. She let her hand slip down over his thigh, and gave him a playful squeeze.

Late that night, Nell suggested they retire to her room. The Bella Union was still going strong, the bar-room and the theater packed with a raucous crowd. On-stage a team of acrobats was performing to assorted hoots and jeers. The audience seemed unimpressed by gymnastic feats of daring.

Denny O'Brien and High Spade McQueen were standing near the end of the bar. The action was heavy at the gaming tables, and they appeared deep in conversation. Starbuck yelled and waved, attracting their attention as Nell tugged him toward the stairs. Mc-Queen barely glanced around, but O'Brien smiled knowingly and gave him the thumbs-up sign. Starbuck responded with a jack-o'-lantern grin, and rolled his eyes at Nell. He looked like a randy drunk, immensely pleased with his prospects for the night.

There was little need for pretense. His head buzzed from the effects of too much champagne, and he was in a very mellow mood. Several bottles of bubbly had been consumed during the evening, and Nell, who was no slouch herself, had matched him glass for glass. She was bright-eyed and giggly, and led him up the staircase with a slight list to her step. Yet, despite his muzzy look, he was reasonably sober. He kept a grin glued on his face, but reminded himself that the night's work had really just begun. He still had to sound Nell out, gull her into revealing a name. And it had to be accomplished without arousing suspicion. Wondering about the best approach, he waved one last time to O'Brien, then trailed Nell up the stairs. The sway of her hips and the glow of the champagne brought him to what seemed a logical compromise. He thought perhaps their talk might wait until after she'd shown him how it was done on the Barbary Coast.

The rooms on the second floor of the Bella Union were reserved for the showgirls. Most of their tricks, ten dollars for five minutes' rutting, were turned on the sofas in the theater boxes. A big spender, who wanted the full treatment, was brought upstairs. There, for the right price, he got to take his time. Fifty dollars bought him an hour, and a hundred purchased the whole night. The girls were versatile, willing to satisfy even the most exotic request, and the johns always got their money's worth. No one left the second floor of the Bella Union wanting more.

The third floor was occupied exclusively by the house staff. Denny O'Brien's suite consisted of a sitting room, bedroom, and private bath. Across the hall, High Spade McQueen's quarters were comparable, though somewhat smaller. Other staff members, who included the stage manager and the house manager, were assigned somewhat less spacious accommodations. Nell occupied a corner room at the end of the hall. The view overlooked the alley.

Upon entering, Starbuck was pleasantly surprised. The atmosphere was considerably more homey than he'd expected. A tall wardrobe, with a full-length mirror, was flanked by a bureau and washstand. Opposite was a grouping of two chairs and a table, upon which stood a gilt clock and a collection of porcelain figurines. The windows were draped, a hooked rug covered the floor, and a large brass bed occupied the far corner. Quite clearly, Nell had gone to great lengths to create a warm and comfortable refuge for herself. The room seemed somehow out of place in the Bella Union.

After locking the door, she turned to Starbuck. Her hands went behind his neck, pulling his head down. Her kiss was fierce and passionate, demanding. She pressed herself against him, and he could feel her breasts and the pressure of her thighs on his loins. He stroked her back and fondled the soft curve of her buttocks, and she uttered a low moan. They parted and, in the umber glow of a lamp, hurriedly began undressing.

Her body was sculptured: high, full breasts, a stemlike waist, and long, shapely legs. She stood before him a moment, her clothes heaped at her feet. Then his arms encircled her, and she clung naked to his hard-muscled frame. Her hand went to his manhood, swollen and pulsating, and she grasped it eagerly. He kissed her lips, then the nape of her neck, felt the nipple of her breast grow erect under his touch. They caressed, played a game of tease-and-tantalize, until they were aroused and aching and the excitement became unbearable. At last, slipping out of his embrace, she pulled him down on the bed.

The hard questing part of him found her. She was ready for him, moist and yielding, and she took him deep within the core of herself. His hands clutched her flanks and they came together in an agonized clash. Her legs spidered around him, and she jolted upward, timing herself to his thrust. She clamped him viselike, her hips moving in a circle, and exhaled a hoarse gasp. He arched his back and drove himself to the molten center, probing deeper and deeper. She screamed and her nails pierced his back like talons.

Time lost meaning, and they crossed the threshold together.

A long while later Starbuck lay staring at the ceiling. Nell was snuggled close, her head nestled in the hollow of his shoulder. He felt her breath eddy through the matted curls on his chest, and sensed she was on the verge of sleep. Champagne and the afterglow of their lovemaking had left her sated, drifting lightly on a quenched flame. He thought there would never be a better time to pop the question. Yet, even with her defenses lowered, he cautioned himself to proceed slowly. He put his lips to her ear and gently stroked her hair.

"Wanna hear a secret?"

"Umm. I like secrets."

Starbuck's voice was warm and husky. "May Ling couldn't hold a candle to you. Strictly no contest, and that's a mortal fact."

"Omigod!" Nell hugged him tightly. "That's the sweetest thing anyone ever said to me in my whole life."

"I meant every word of it—cross my heart."

"Does that mean you'll stay out of Chinatown?"

"Would that make you happy?"

"Would it ever!" Nell's eyes suddenly shone, and she laughed. "Why, it would make that little pigeontoed bitch turn pea-green with envy!"

"Consider it done," Starbuck said with a beguiling grin. "Chinatown's seen the last of Harry Lovett."

"You won't regret it." Nell squirmed around and kissed him soundly. "I'll keep you so worn out you won't have strength enough to eat."

"Hell, why not!" Starbuck chuckled and settled back on the pillow, watching her a moment. "Now that I've told you my secret, you tell me yours."

"Ask away." Nell gave him a sassy, nose-wrinkling smile. "I've already shown you most of my secrets, anyway."

"Well—" Starbuck hesitated, his features sober. "I was wondering why you're afraid of Denny O'Brien."

"Denny?" Surprise washed over Nell's face. "What gave you the idea I'm afraid of Denny?"

"Aren't you?"

"Not on your tintype! Denny's not nearly as tough as he puts on. Besides, if he ever tried any rough stuff with me, he knows I'd take a hike. And p.d.q. too!"

"You could've fooled me."

"Honeybunch, you just lost me. Fooled you when?"

"Earlier tonight," Starbuck replied, "when I asked you why Denny hasn't taken over Chinatown. You clammed up tighter than a drum."

"So what?"

"So I'd say you're scared of him. Damn good and scared!"

"No——" Nell's voice skipped a beat. "Not Denny."

"Who, then?"

"The blind . . ."

Her words trailed away, and she stiffened in his arms. Starbuck studied her with open curiosity. "Go ahead, finish it. The blind ——— ?"

There was an awkward pause. "Harry, take some good advice. While you're in Frisco, don't ask too many questions. What you don't know can't hurt you."

"That bad, huh?"

"You just take my word for it . . . okay?"

"Hell, forget I asked!" Starbuck laughed jovially. "No skin off my nose."

"And let's keep it that way." Nell burrowed deeper into the hollow of his shoulder. "I like your nose just the way it is."

Starbuck dropped it there. He knew he'd learned all he would for one night, and there was no need to push it further. He pulled her to him in a tight embrace, saying no more. Yet the words stuck in his mind, and he found himself genuinely baffled. He lay very still, silently repeating something that seemed to make no sense.

The blind . . .

Chapter Nine

"Tell me about Mr. Lovett."

"I do not trust him, master."

"Please explain."

May Ling was seated across the table from Fung Jing Toy. A hatchet man had escorted her into his chambers only moments ago. Earlier that afternoon, when the one named Harry Lovett had departed her lodgings, she knew she would be summoned to the house on Washington Street. She had spent the balance of the afternoon in deep reflection, artfully phrasing the report she would deliver to her master. Now, under Fung's benign gaze, she began what seemed to her a perilous journey. She dared not to be wrong.

"I believe he is an imposter." Her voice was soft and troubled. "One who pretends to be what he is not."

Fung stared at her in a mild abstracted way. "Did he abuse you?"

"No, master," May Ling said quickly. "He was very gentle for a *fan kwei*."

"How did he differ from other white men I have sent to you?"

"He was not impatient or crude. Nor was he cruel in his demands. We joined three times during the night, and each time he took me without harshness. Today, when we returned from the auction, we joined once again. He was even more considerate . . . gentle."

Fung weighed her words a moment. The white devils, even the wealthy ones, were renowned for their coarse sexual habits and their lack of sophistication in bed. Yet, just as there were brutal Chinese, so might there be gentle white men. To think in absolutes was to cloud one's judgment.

"So then," he said quietly. "Your suspicion was aroused because he did not treat you in the manner practiced by white men?"

"I thought it strange, master. You told me his plan was to open several brothels, and such men are known for their barbaric customs. He was not what I expected."

"Very well," Fung nodded. "Mr. Lovett apparently has attributes uncommon to brothelkeepers. Is there more?"

"Yes, master," May Ling noted seriously. "His behavior at the auction was most revealing."

"You followed my instructions?"

"Oh yes! As you ordered, I asked no questions and gave him no reason for alarm. When I suggested attending the auction, he was very excited, very curious. He believed it was something I had thought of only then. A small inspiration to make his tour of Little China more enjoyable."

"What happened then?"

"At the auction, I observed him closely. His curiosity quickly turned to an attitude of disapproval. He held his tongue, but it was there to see, nonetheless. He frowned, and suddenly became very thoughtful."

"Perhaps he is a thoughtful man."

"Perhaps," May Ling said tactfully. "Quite, soon, however, a circumstance arose which allowed me to test him. I led him into a discussion of slave girls who are unsuitable for auction. His questions enabled me to speak of conditions in the cribs . . . and the hospital."

"Ah!" A pinpoint of light glittered in Fung's eyes. "You trapped him!"

"I merely deceived him, master. He betrayed himself."

"In what way?"

"He was shocked," May Ling remarked. "When I explained how the crib girls end their days, his expression was one of loathing. The very idea of the hospital was abhorrent to him."

"He told you that?"

"Not in words," May Ling said, her eyes downcast. "I sensed it, master. His reaction was that of a white devil missionary. He felt sadness and compassion for the crib girls."

"We were informed that this is his first venture as a brothelkeeper. According to O'Brien, he was what the whites call a con man. Perhaps he has not yet acquired the dispassionate nature necessary to such work."

"Certain things cannot be hidden, master. Whatever his designs are, the man named Lovett is not what he claims. He is an impostor."

"You speak now of intuition, things you devine rather than fact itself. Is it not so?"

"A woman knows," May Ling said, looking directly at him. "How she knows cannot be explained, but that makes it no less real. This man is dangerous, and I fear he will bring evil to your house. I must say what I believe to be true, master."

For a protracted interval, Fung was silent. He steepled his fingers together, considering both the girl and her statement. She was young, but wise beyond her years. Several times in the past he had used her to gain insight into men who sought to do business with him. Her intuition was a mystic thing, and a force not to be regarded lightly. Then, too, everything she'd told him merely served to reinforce his own sense of disquiet. Something about Lovett bothered him, and it was for that reason he had arranged the liaison with May Ling. He examined the alternatives, and quickly decided to heed her warning. The sale of a hundred virgins was, after all, a thing of no great consequence.

"I have learned," he said at length, "that Mr. Lovett will sleep with O'Brien's whore tonight."

"Nothing escapes you, master."

"Quite so," Fung agreed loftily. "I have eyes everywhere, even in the Bella Union."

"Will the Kimball woman also attempt deception?"

"No," Fung said without inflection. "O'Brien is blinded by greed. He suspects nothing."

"A shame," May Ling commented slyly. "But then, no *fan kwei* could be expected to have your wisdom and foresight."

A wintry smile lighted Fung's eyes. "You have performed the task well, and I am pleased."

"I live only to serve you, master."

"Leave me now. Other matters require my attention."

May Ling obediently rose, placed her hands together, and dipped low in a bow. She stepped backward to the door, then turned and walked past the dogs. Fung snapped his fingers, and one of the hatchet men appeared in the doorway. He took pen and paper off the table, and laboriously scrawled a note in English. Then he folded it and looked up at the waiting hatchet man.

"You will deliver this message to the blind white devil."

The Snug Café was located on O'Farrell Street, in the heart of the Uptown Tenderloin. Shortly before midnight, a closed carriage rolled to a halt in the alleyway behind the café. Wong Yee and Sing Dock stepped out of the carriage and inspected the alley in both directions. There was no one in sight.

The hatchet men assisted Fung down from the carriage. He walked directly to the back door of the café and knocked. He was expected, and the door swung open almost instantly. Knuckles Jackson, a pugnosed bruiser who served as bouncer, waved him through and closed the door. Wong Yee and Sing Dock exchanged a look. Only here would the master dispense with their services and enter unguarded. Neither of them thought the order odd, for only here was he safe without them. Still, it did nothing to lessen their concern.

Inside, Knuckles Jackson led Fung through a storage room and up a flight of stairs. There he stopped and rapped twice on a door. A muffled voice responded and he ushered Fung into a lavishly appointed office. The furniture was black walnut, intricately carved, and upholstered in plush velvet. Logs crackled in a black marble fireplace, and a crystal lamp bathed the room in dim light. Beyond the fireplace, cloaked in shadow, stood a massive walnut desk.

The man seated behind the desk was in his early fifties. He wore a frock coat and striped trousers, and a black cravat with a pearl stickpin. His features were lean and angular, and his gray hair was complimented by a neatly trimmed mustache. His eyes were all but invisible behind dark tinted glasses. He gestured toward a chair, and smiled.

"Do come in, Fung. Have a seat."

"Thank you, Mr. Buckley." Fung took the chair, folding his hands in his lap. "It was kind of you to see me on such short notice."

"Not at all." Buckley dismissed Knuckles Jackson with a nod, and waited until the door closed. "Now, what can I do for you? I daresay it's nothing inconsequential at this late hour."

"That is so." Fung's tone was curiously deferential. "A problem has arisen, and I felt it should be brought to your attention immediately."

"Well, well, that does sound serious. Suppose you tell me about it."

"I regret to say it involves Denny O'Brien."

"Oh?" The smile faded and a shadow of irritation crossed Buckley's features. "I trust you and Denny aren't at one another's throats again?"

"I have not overstepped my boundaries. To my knowledge, neither has O'Brien. As you directed, we have worked together in a spirit of cooperation."

"And now?"

"There is no dispute with regard to territory. O'Brien confines himself to the Barbary Coast, and I do the same in Chinatown. In that respect, we have both honored your wishes."

"Diplomacy has its place, but let's dispense with it for the moment, shall we? Please come to the point."

"Yes, of course," Fung said promptly. "O'Brien sent a man to me three days ago on a business matter. I now have reason—"

"A white man?"

"Indeed, so," Fung said with no trace of resentment.

"A white man by the name of Harry Lovett, who purports to be a whoremaster from Colorado."

"Very well. Please go on."

"I now have reason to believe Lovett is not what he claims."

"Not a whoremaster?"

"Precisely."

"What is he, then?"

"I have no idea." Fung offered an elaborate shrug. "Because the situation is confused, I thought it wise to seek your counsel."

Buckley sighed, tilting back in his chair. "In the interest of time, why not start at the beginning? And please, Fung, spare me the details. Stick to essentials, the bare bones."

The reproach was delivered in a condescending tone. Fung, who suddenly felt very Oriental and very much out of his element, evidenced no offense. Instead, he launched into a straightforward account of the past three days. He outlined O'Brien's role as intermediary, and went on to describe his meeting with Lovett. He dwelled at length on the matter of a hundred virgins, and Lovett's unusually quick acceptance of the asking price. With a certain flair for intrigue, he then recounted May Ling's role in the affair, and the sequence of events leading to the slave-girl auction. He concluded with a summation of May Ling's misgivings, adding that he, too, shared her doubts. There he paused and awaited Buckley's reaction.

"Are you telling me you're relying solely on this girl's intuition . . . her feelings about Lovett?"

"To a large extent," Fung admitted. "She has great insight into men, and her perceptions have never failed me before."

Buckley's look was colored by skepticism. "A bit like

reading tea leaves, isn't it? You really have nothing con-
crete to support your view."

"I am satisfied." Fung's features grew overcast. "I no
longer wish to do business with this man Lovett."

"What harm could come of it? We have the fix in
with immigration, so he's obviously not a government
agent. I fail to see how he poses a threat."

"A threat assumes many guises. I have no way of
knowing who Lovett may or may not be. On the other
hand, I do know the value of caution. I would prefer to
cancel the arrangement without delay."

Buckley appeared to lose interest. "Do as you please.
Simply inform Lovett the deal's off."

"There are other considerations," Fung said in a
musing voice. "O'Brien has quite probably charged
Lovett a middleman's fee. That places me in an awkward position."

"Exactly what is it you're asking?"

"I wish you to intercede on my behalf. O'Brien will
accept your judgment, and the matter will end there."

"I dislike getting involved in these petty squabbles.
Good God, you and Denny are grown men! Work it out
for yourselves."

Fung gave him a straight, hard look. "As you are
aware, O'Brien bears me personal ill will, and he also
covets Chinatown. Were I to withdraw from this arrangement—thereby causing him financial loss—he
might easily use it as a pretext to start trouble. Without
your intercession, our spirit of harmony may very well
be jeopardized. I urge you to reconsider."

"In short," Buckley said with heavy sarcasm, "you
want me to pull your chestnuts out of the fire?"

"I bow to your wisdom at all times. As you have so
often reminded me—you are the boss."

Buckley gave the matter some thought. "Very well,"

he said finally, "I'll look into it. I want you to understand something, though. When you make your problems my problems, I begin wondering if maybe I don't need myself a new boy in Chinatown. You might reflect on that before you come begging favors again."

"I most humbly apologize." Fung rose and bowed slightly from the waist. "I wish only to maintain the peace and prosperity we enjoy under your guidance."

"Good night, Fung. I'll let you know what happens."

Buckley sat perfectly still until the door closed. Then he removed his glasses and massaged his eyes. He was tired and his head ached, and at times like tonight, he felt very much like a rooster atop a dung heap. The footing somehow never seemed all that firm. Nor had he yet accustomed himself to the smell.

Denny O'Brien was summoned late the next morning. The Snug Café wasn't yet open for business, but he, too, entered through the alley door. Upstairs, he kept his greeting short and polite, and dropped into a chair before the desk. Buckley went straight to the point.

"Fung paid me a visit last night. He's jumpy about a deal you arranged with some fellow named Lovett."

"What d'you mean?" O'Brien said with an annoyed squint. "What's there to be jumpy about?"

"He want's out," Buckley said flatly. "He seems to think your friend Lovett isn't on the up and up."

"That's crazy!" O'Brien burst out. "Harry Lovett's as square as they come!"

"What makes you think so?"

"Mattie Silks herself sent him to see me. She's the biggest madam in Denver, and anyone she recommends is ace-high in my book."

Buckley looked somber. "Have you checked him out? Wired Mattie Silks or some of our friends in Denver?"

"No." O'Brien shook his head in exasperation. "Why would I check him out? Jesus H. Christ, the man's loaded! He's ready to hand Fung a hundred thousand —for virgins, no less!"

"And I take it you've cut yourself in for a piece of the action?"

"Why not?" O'Brien bridled. "I made the introduction, didn't I?"

"Perhaps that's the problem." Buckley's tone was severe. "I got the distinct impression Fung suspects you slipped a ringer in on him. He's convinced Lovett is a setup of some sort."

"Goddamn him!" O'Brien roared vindictively. "That slant-eyed little son-of-a-bitch never stops! He won't be satisfied till I'm six feet under and turned into worm meat."

"Have you given him reason?"

"Hell, no! You laid out the rules and I've stayed on my side of the street. Chinatown don't mean beans to me."

"Then why would he turn leery so quickly? From what he told me, it sounds like a fairly routine deal."

"It's spite, plain and simple." O'Brien face congealed into a scowl. "He's willing to queer the deal just to give everybody a laugh at my expense. That makes him look like a big man to all his Chink pals."

"I think not." Buckley's headshake was slow and emphatic. "His concern was genuine. He believes there's something fishy, and he would sooner be safe than sorry."

"By Jesus!" O'Brien said stubbornly. "I won't hold still for it. I stood to make a cool ten thousand on this deal, and I mean to have it."

"You're wrong." Buckley's voice was suddenly edged. "You'll do exactly what I tell you to do, Denny. I won't allow you or anyone else to upset my applecart. Do I make myself clear?"

"I hear you," O'Brien said grudgingly. "But it goes down hard, you taking that slope-head's side against me."

"Wrong again," Buckley replied with weary tolerance. "I haven't ruled one way or the other, not yet."

"I don't get you."

"It occurs to me that Mr. Lovett and I should have a talk. You bring him around late this evening. I'll make my judgment then, and it won't have anything to do with you or Fung. All very impartial, based strictly on my impression of Lovett."

"Little risky, isn't it?" O'Brien looked worried. "He's no dummy, and you're not exactly somebody he'd forget real quick."

Buckley's laugh was strange and somehow cryptic. "Our talk might prove risky for Mr. Lovett. Only time and the tea leaves will tell."

O'Brien felt a tingle along his backbone. He'd heard that laugh before, and he knew precisely what it meant. Tonight there would be no quibbling, no questions left unanswered. Nor would there be anything remotely resembling a second chance.

Harry Lovett was a dead man unless he passed muster.

Chapter Ten

It was half-past eight when Starbuck arrived at the Bella Union. He reeked of rosewood lotion and was attired in yet another of his spiffy outfits. He walked through the barroom and paused in the doorway of the theater. Thumbs hooked in his vest, he slowly scanned the crowd.

His appointment with Nell was for somewhere around nine. Their plans, with one exception, were much the same as last night. A theater box was reserved, chilled champagne was on order, and the first part of their evening would be devoted to the early show. Afterward, a late supper would be served in the privacy of Nell's room. The balance of the night, something of a return engagement, would be spent in bed. There would be lovemaking and talk, lots of talk. Tonight, he expected to learn considerably more about San Francisco's underworld. Perhaps all he needed to know.

Standing in the doorway, he thought it strange that Nell was nowhere in sight. He glanced at the curtained box and saw that it was empty. Then, checking his watch, it occurred to him that she might still be in her room. He was about to turn when High Spade McQueen laid a hand on his shoulder. He looked around.

"The boss wants to see you." McQueen jerked his chin toward the staircase. "Now."

"Why sure thing, High Spade. Lead the way."

Something in McQueen's attitude alerted him. When they reached the staircase, any lingering doubt was dispelled. McQueen casually lagged behind and followed him, rather than leading him up the stairs. He knew then he was in trouble. He warned himself to go slow and keep a sharp lookout.

On the balcony, McQueen opened the office door and motioned him through. Denny O'Brien was seated behind the desk, his expression grim. Starbuck heard the door close, and realized he was sandwiched between them. With a jaunty air, he flipped O'Brien a salute and approached the desk.

"Evening, Denny," he said with a jocular smile. "How's tricks?"

O'Brien's hand appeared from beneath the desk, holding a pistol. "Don't make any sudden moves."

"Judas Priest!" Starbuck croaked. "What the hell's the idea?"

"Shut your trap." O'Brien looked past him. "Mac, pat him down."

McQueen expertly went over him. The Colt Lightning was discovered almost immediately, and removed from its shoulder holster. His arms were checked for a sleeve gun; then his waistband and all his pockets were thoroughly searched. He waited, certain the hideout gun in his boot top was next; but his legs weren't touched. Finally, McQueen shoved him into a chair and looked across at O'Brien.

"He's clean."

"You're sure he hasn't got a hideout?"

"One peashooter." McQueen palmed the Colt and stuck it inside his belt. "That's it, boss."

O'Brien laid his pistol on the desk. Then, with a venomous glare, his gaze shifted to Starbuck. "I oughta bust your goddamn skull wide open."

"For Chrissake!" Starbuck said, squirming around in his chair. "What's the matter? What'd I do?"

"I'll ask the questions!" O'Brien's first slammed onto the desk. "You just gimme some straight answers, or else I'll let Mac and his sailor pals feed you to the sharks."

"Anything at all, Denny. Go ahead, ask away."

"How come you told me you're in thick with the sporting crowd in Denver?"

"I never said that," Starbuck corrected him. "I told you I mostly worked the mining camps. All I said about Denver was that me and Mattie Silks are on good terms."

"You're a liar!" O'Brien shouted. "I wired Mattie and she said she never heard of you."

"That's a crock," Starbuck said stoutly. "No way on God's green earth Mattie wouldn't vouch for me."

He saw he'd guessed right. O'Brien's eyes gave him away, and he quickly backed off from the bluff. "All right, so I wired her and just haven't got the answer yet. It amounts to the same thing. If she don't give you a clean bill of health, you'll get deep-sixed so fast you won't know what hit you."

"Denny, I'll give you odds on what her wire says."

"Don't get too cocky," O'Brien warned him. "You've still got your balls in a nutcracker."

"What's that supposed to mean?"

"Suppose you tell me about your talk with Fung."

"Fung?" Starbuck looked bewildered. "Hell, there wasn't much talk to it. He set a price, and we dickered for a while, then I finally agreed. That's the way we left it."

"You had a deal, then? You're sure of that?"

"I'm plumb sure. No two ways about it."

"When did he say he'd make delivery?"

"Well . . ." Starbuck stopped, thoughtful a moment. "He didn't say, not exactly. He allowed it would take a while to get that many virgins together, and told me he'd be in touch."

"How long? A week, two weeks?"

"He never spelled it out, and I never asked. I'd already agreed to pay top dollar, so I figured he'd hop right to it."

"Didn't it ever occur to you that you might be getting the run-around?"

"Why would he do a thing like that?"

"Forget it," O'Brien muttered. "What did he ask you about me?"

"Nothing." Starbuck shrugged, shook his head. "Near as I recollect, your name wasn't even mentioned."

O'Brien gave him a swift, intense look. "Think back on it, real hard. Maybe he asked you how long we've known each other? Whether or not we've done business before? Anything along that line?"

"Not a word," Starbuck said without hesitation. "Course, he seemed to know all about me and what it was I wanted. I just naturally assumed you'd managed to fill him in before I got there."

"You assumed right." O'Brien mulled it over briefly, then glanced up. "What about the girl, May Ling? She mention me, try to draw you out somehow?"

"Same story," Starbuck observed. "She never said

boo about anything except Chinatown and the slave-girl trade."

"Yeah, that's right. She took you to the auction, didn't she? Cooked you a Chink meal and screwed your ears off—and never asked one question about me! Is that what you're saying?"

"That's the works, Denny. Start to finish."

O'Brien's voice suddenly turned querulous. "You stupid son-of-a-bitch! Do you think I'm gonna sit here and let you con me like some snot-nosed hayseed?"

"Con you?" Starbuck was genuinely surprised. "I'm telling it to you straight. Honest to Christ!"

"Bullshit!" O'Brien glowered back at him. "I happen to know you asked Nell how come I never tried to take over Chinatown."

"So?"

"So where'd you dream up that idea? I'll tell you where! Fung and that little Chinee bitch put the bee in your ear. The whole time you were with 'em, they pumped you dry about me, didn't they?"

"No, goddamnit, they didn't!" Starbuck sounded indignant. "I told it to you just the way it happened."

"Then why'd you ask Nell what you did?"

"Because any fool could see you and Fung hate each other's guts. Nobody has to say anything! It's plain as a diamond in a goat's ass."

"And you figured it out all by yourself?"

"Hell, yes!" Starbuck blustered. "Fung and his hatchet men wouldn't be any match for you and your boys. That's plain to see, too. I guess it just got my curiosity working overtime."

"Curiosity about what?"

"Well, I don't mean to insult you, Denny. But, Jesus Christ, nobody's got your arms tied, have they? The way it looks to me, you could've gobbled up Chinatown anytime you took a notion. It's like I told Nell—if it was me, there wouldn't be no way I could resist giving it a try."

O'Brien's silence was all the answer Starbuck needed. He sensed Nell had lied. She hadn't told O'Brien about his greater curiosity, the vague questions he'd asked about an underworld kingpin. Nor had she mentioned her own slip of the tongue, her unfinished statement that ended abruptly with "the blind." Quite clearly, she had lied to protect him. Whether she realized it or not, she had nudged herself a step closer to his side of the line. He now had something approaching an ally in the enemy camp. A little softsoap, with a dash of blackmail added, would soon bring her around.

O'Brien, who seemed to have recovered his humor, finally broke the silence. "Harry, I'll have to hand it to you. You're a pretty smooth article."

"Why, thank you, Denny. I'm sort of sweet on you, too."

"Don't misunderstand me," O'Brien countered. "You're not out of the woods yet."

"Oh, how so?"

"Well, as it happens, we've got a helluva problem with Fung. He wants to back out on the deal. Somehow or other, he's turned leery toward you."

"Why?" Starbuck demanded. "What's his reason?"

"I'm not altogether sure," O'Brien said, frowning. "From what I gather, he's got it in his head you're working with me—a swindle of some sort—or else you're a government agent."

"He's nuts!" Starbuck scoffed. "I don't work for you or anyone else. And that goddamned sure includes the government!"

"All the same, that's what we're up against."

"Then we'll just wait till you get Mattie's wire. Once

you show him that, he'll know I'm on the level and we're back in business."

"Harry, if it was up to me, I wouldn't hesitate a minute. But it's out of my hands now."

Starbuck's pulse quickened. "I don't get your meaning."

"You've got an appointment." O'Brien rose and stuffed his pistol in the waistband of his trousers. "Tonight you're to talk with the big man himself, Mr. Frisco."

"Mr. Frisco?"

"Let's get a move on. You're expected, and I wouldn't care to keep him waiting."

With O'Brien in the lead, and McQueen bringing up the rear, they went through the door and crossed the balcony. On the way down the stairs, Starbuck was acutely aware that his gun had not been returned. He also understood, though it was left unspoken, that he had passed only Denny O'Brien's test.

Mr. Frisco, and a sterner test, was yet to come.

A gentle rain was falling as the carriage turned off O'Farrell Street. Starbuck wasn't at all surprised that their destination was located in the Uptown Tenderloin. His theory regarding the boss of San Francisco's underworld was now confirmed.

All the way uptown he had tried in vain to learn the identity of Mr. Frisco. His questions finally provoked Denny O'Brien, and he was told to drop the subject. Still, with or without a name, it was clear O'Brien and Fung answered to one man. A man who rubbed elbows with the city's social elite, the rich and the powerful. A mastermind who had created a brilliant cover, disassociating himself completely from Chinatown and the

Barbary Coast. And therefore a man who was exceedingly dangerous.

The thought was foremost in Starbuck's mind as the carriage rolled to a halt in the alleyway. He knew the next few minutes would determine whether he lived or died. Mr. Frisco had gone to great lengths to conceal his identity. Yet he apparently had no qualms about exposing himself to a Colorado whoremaster. The conclusion was obvious, and the hazard involved was beyond question. Unless Mr. Frisco got all the right answers, the end result was chillingly simple to predict. One whoremaster, more or less, would never be missed.

The alley door opened and Knuckles Jackson waved them inside. Starbuck was treated to yet another search, but took scant comfort from the fact that his hideout gun once again went undetected. McQueen and Jackson, who belonged to the same brotherhood of gorillas, remained on guard in the storeroom. O'Brien escorted him up the stairs, which meant he was covered front and rear. The chances of shooting his way out weren't even worth calculating. His wits were now his only hope for survival.

The light in the office was dim, and the man behind the desk sat immobile. Starbuck had the fleeting impression of a store-window dummy propped up in a chair. Then O'Brien closed the door, removing his hat, and walked forward. Starbuck followed suit, quickly inspecting the office. The door to the storeroom stairs was the only exit.

"Here he is," O'Brien said, halting in front of the desk. "Harry Lovett."

"Thank you, Denny." Buckley made a small gesture of dismissal. "Wait downstairs. I'll call if I need you."

O'Brien seemed on the verge of questioning the order. Then he bobbed his head, turning away, and crossed the office. A moment later the door closed. Starbuck grinned and stuck out his hand.

"Pleased to meet you, Mr. Frisco."

Starbuck was rocked by a sudden jolt of awareness. His arm extended, leaning over the desk, he got his first good look at the man. The face was a living waxwork, and behind the dark tinted glasses, the eyes were marble-like. He had the eerie sensation of gazing into the eyes of a stuffed animal, glassy and unmoving. Nell's word's flitted through his head, and abruptly it all made sense. The blind man! She'd almost blurted it out, and now he saw it for himself. The boss of San Francisco's underworld was *blind*. His mouth popped open and he slowly withdrew his hand. He stood there, too stunned to speak.

"Have a seat, Mr. Lovett." Buckley motioned him to a chair. "I presume it was Denny who referred to me as Mr. Frisco?"

"Yeah." Starbuck took a seat, rapidly collected his wits. "He said it was all the name I needed to know."

"By no means," Buckley said with a frosty smile. "My name is Buckley. Christopher Buckley."

"Well, Mr. Buckley, maybe you can explain something to me. What's all this strongarm business about? I came out here to buy myself some whores, and now I've got people sticking guns in my face."

"I'm afraid Denny overreacts at times. You see, Mr. Lovett, we have a difference of opinion with respect to the girls you wish to purchase. I've been asked to arbitrate the matter."

"You're talking about Fung trying to welch on our deal?"

"Exactly." Buckley inclined his head in a faint nod. "In Fung's words, you are not what you represent yourself to be, Mr. Lovett."

"So Denny told me." Starbuck switched to a light and mocking tone. "Dumb goddamn Chinaman! Somebody ought to tell him he's got his head screwed on backward."

"Perhaps you wouldn't mind answering a question?"

"Fire away," Starbuck said cheerfully. "I've got no secrets."

"Are you familiar with Lou Blomger?"

"Why, hell, yes! Everybody in Denver knows Lou Blomger. You name it, he runs it! The rackets, politics —the whole ball of wax."

"I wired him this morning." Buckley indicated a telegram lying open on the desk. "If you care to read his reply, he says in no uncertain terms he never heard of Harry Lovett."

"What's that prove?" Starbuck protested. "Blomger's out of my league. I work the mining camps, not Denver. He wouldn't know me from Adam's off ox."

"Come now, Mr. Lovett. A man with your connections—Mattie Silks, no less—and Blomger never heard of you. I find that difficult to believe."

Starbuck took a chance. "Tell you what, Mr. Buckley. You're so fond of sending wires, send one to Bailey Youngston in Leadville. He owns the Texas House Saloon and half the town to boot. Ask him if I didn't knock down the biggest score of my life, not two months ago, sitting right in his joint. Hell, for the right price, he'll even tell you the sucker's name!"

There was a long silence. "Very well, Mr. Lovett," Buckley said at length. "I will defer my decision for the moment—but only on three conditions. One, we will await replies from Mattie Silks and your friend, Youngston. Next, as a gesture of good faith, you will deposit one hundred thousand dollars in the bank of my choice by closing time tomorrow. Will that present any problem?"

"No problem at all," Starbuck assured him earnestly. "I came prepared to pay in cash, so you just name your bank and I'll be there johnny-on-the-spot."

"Fine," Buckley said with dungeon calm. "I feel quite certain that will go a long way toward dispelling Fung's apprehension."

"You said there were three conditions?"

"Indeed, I did." A cold smile touched the corner of Buckley's mouth. "Until the matter is resolved to my satisfaction, you will make no attempt to leave San Francisco. Need I elaborate on that condition further?"

"No, sir, no need. I get your drift completely."

Starbuck knew he'd been given a reprieve, nothing more. Bailey Youngston was the owner of the Texas House Saloon, but nobody in Leadville had ever heard of Harry Lovett. Youngston might answer a wire from a stranger, and he might not. That was a toss-up, and could go either way. The money, on the other hand, was a surefire certainty. And tomorrow at closing time was less than twenty-four hours away.

All of a sudden Starbuck felt like a juggler with one too many balls in the air. Yet there was no question which one he had to grab first, and fastest.

He wondered where the hell he could lay his hands on $100,000!

Chapter Eleven

Nell was waiting in the theater box. The Bella Union was already packed, but she easily spotted them as they moved through the crowd in the barroom. O'Brien paused near the staircase, talking with Starbuck a moment. Then, accompanied by High Spade McQueen, he mounted the stairs and disappeared into his office.

Starbuck looked toward the box and saw her. Doffing his hat, he waved, smiling broadly. She waved back, watching as he crossed the theater and went up the short flight of stairs leading to the loge. Earlier, one of the bartenders had told her he'd left the Bella Union with O'Brien and McQueen. She had no idea where they had gone or why. Nor was she about to ask. Their business dealings were none of her concern, and she preferred to keep it that way. Experience had taught her that inquisitive women often learned too much for their own good. In her view, she was paid to entertain, not ask questions.

"Sorry I'm late."

Entering the box, Starbuck tossed his hat on the sofa

and took a chair beside her. Nell gave him a dazzling smile, and leaned forward to kiss him lightly on the mouth.

"No need to apologize, lover. You're here now, and that's what counts."

"We still set to have supper in your room?"

"Of course." She removed a bottle of champagne from an ice bucket and filled two glasses. "What's an hour more or less? The night's young."

"That's my girl!" Starbuck winked and lifted his glass in a toast. "Here's mud in your eye."

Nell laughed, clinking glasses. "Yours, too, honey-bun."

Starbuck appraised her as she sipped champagne. He detected a false note in her voice and saw the guarded look in her eyes. He seriously doubted that O'Brien had confided in her, or told her that a meeting had been arranged with Buckley. Yet she was curious, and clearly biting her tongue not to ask questions. He thought to himself that it was a good sign. Her curiosity made her vulnerable.

Handled properly, tonight's development could accomplish two essential goals. She might easily be guiled into revealing more about Buckley, and his place in the scheme of things. With time at a premium, any scrap of information was vital, and she represented the only dependable source. Further, the more she revealed, the simpler it would be to enlist her as an ally. By playing on her curiosity, and her fear of O'Brien, she might be forced into a conspiracy from which there was no return. A certain risk was attached, but he really had no choice. Tonight would determine whether or not he could trust her, and exactly how far she would go in the event push came to shove. All that remained was to sound her out.

Tossing off his champagne, he refilled their glasses. Then, a thumb hooked in his vest, he sat back and grinned expansively.

"So far it's been some night."

"Oh?"

"Yessir, it has for a fact. Denny introduced me to the big boy himself, in the flesh."

"The big boy?"

"The blind man." Starbuck watched her out of the corner of his eye. "Christopher Buckley."

Surprise washed over Nell's face. "Denny took you to see Buckley?"

"Sure did," Starbuck said carelessly. "Had ourselves a pretty nice chat, too."

Nell nodded, then smiled a little. "You're going up in the world. Not many people get to meet Mr. Buckley."

"You mean to say you've never met him?"

"Nooo," she said slowly. "He's out of my league."

"Then how'd you know he was blind?"

"Blind?"

"Yeah." Starbuck idly gestured with his champagne glass. "Last night you started to say something about the blind somebody or other, but you never finished it."

"I was talking out of turn. I didn't know Denny had arranged a meeting."

"Tell you the truth, I don't think Denny arranged anything."

Nell gave him a glance full of curiosity. "I'm not sure I understand."

"Well—" Starbuck took a sip of champagne, pondered a moment. "Unless I read it wrong, when Buckley say frog, Denny squats. Am I right or not?"

"You're close enough."

"Thought so." Starbuck bobbed his head sagely.

"Buckley ordered him to bring me around all because of that damn fool Chinaman."

"Fung?"

"Nothing serious." Starbuck rocked his hand, fingers splayed. "Fung evidently got cold feet about our deal. Had some asinine notion that Denny and me were out to gaff him somehow."

Nell looked upset. "You mean Buckley thought you weren't on the level?"

"The way he put it, he'd been asked to arbitrate the matter. That's fancy lingo for saying it's up to him whether or not the deal goes through."

"What happened?"

"Won't know for a couple of days," Starbuck observed casually. "He wants to check out my references before he decides, and I told him that was fine by me. Harry Lovett's got nothing to hide."

"You're sure of that?" Nell asked anxiously. "Buckley's one man you don't want for an enemy."

Starbuck uttered a low chuckle. "I got the same impression myself. Denny acted like he was in the presence of Jesus Christ and the Lord God Jehovah all rolled into one."

"You're getting warm, lover. So far as this town's concerned, anyway."

"Now that you mention it," Starbuck appeared thoughtful, "on the way uptown, Denny called him 'Mr. Frisco.' I reckon the name fits, or else Denny and Fung wouldn't report to him like good little soldiers."

"Denny told you that?"

"Told me what?"

"About reporting to Buckley?"

"Nope," Starbuck readily admitted. "But it's plain enough to see. Denny and Fung are like lieutenants; one runs the Coast and the other runs Chinatown.

Buckley cracks the whip, and whatever hoop he holds up, that's the one they jump through."

"I wouldn't say that out loud too often if I were you."

"Why?" Starbuck looked at her directly. "It's the truth, isn't it?"

Nell averted her gaze. A troupe of acrobats went tumbling across the stage, and she watched them in silence for a time. Finally, with a furtive shrug, she spoke in a low voice.

"Harry, the truth can get you hurt. Take some good advice, and don't let anybody know you've figured out how things work in Frisco."

"Yeah, I suppose you're right."

"I know I'm right."

"All the same, there's one thing that damn sure doesn't figure."

"You'll ask anyway," Nell said reluctantly, "so go ahead."

"How the hell's a blind man put the fear of God in someone like Denny O'Brien?"

"I'll give you three guesses, and the first two don't count."

"You make it sound awful simple."

"Nothing simpler, if you have the stomach for it."

Starbuck smiled. "How about a clue?"

"Oh, suppose we call it the second oldest profession in the world?"

The curtain at the door opened and O'Brien stepped into the box. He nodded to Nell, his mouth split in a wide smile. Then he moved around the sofa and genially clapped Starbuck on the shoulder.

"Enjoying the show?"

"Which one?"

"Which one?" O'Brien parroted, gesturing toward the stage. "I only see one."

"Oh, that?" Starbuck rolled his eyes at Nell. "Just between you and me, Denny, I'm waiting for the finale."

"Harry, you're a sport! Goddamn me if you aren't."

"Let's just say there are other things I prefer to acrobats."

"You'll be spending the night with us, then?"

Starback looked at him, unable to guess what might be going through his mind. The question was phrased in the manner of an invitation, but there was an undertone of command in O'Brien's voice. Whether the message was meant for Starbuck or Nell seemed a moot point. The owner of the Bella Union hadn't popped into the box to make small talk. He was there for a purpose.

"Nell's the one to ask." Starbuck let go a hoot of laughter. "I can go all night and then some, but a girl needs her beauty sleep."

"Don't worry about Nell," O'Brien advised with heavy good humor. "She's lots tougher than she looks."

"I'll let you know in the morning."

"You do that, Harry."

O'Brien grinned, as if at some private joke. Then he glanced at Nell and turned away. The curtain parted and they were once more alone in the box.

Starbuck poured champagne, seemingly unperturbed by the interruption. He noted that Nell's manner was pensive and oddly taut. Her gaze was fixed on the stage. He gave her leg a squeeze and chortled softly to himself.

"That Denny's a card, isn't he? Always funning around—"

"You lied to me!"

"Lied?" Starbuck feigned astonishment. "What the hell are you talking about?"

"Stop it!" Nell said in a shaky voice. "You're trying to con me, and I don't appreciate it one damn bit."

"You got a crystal ball, or did you figure that out all by yourself?"

"I don't need a crystal ball. I know Denny like the back of my hand, and he wasn't playing patty-cake and roses. He came up here to give you a warning."

Starbuck smiled lamely and lifted his hands in a shrug. "You've got me dead to rights. I needed help and I wasn't exactly sure how to go about asking."

"What kind of help?"

"I'm caught in the middle," Starbuck lied, straight-faced. "Denny and Fung are out to axe one another, and they're using me as a stalking horse. That's what brought Buckley into it. He doesn't want any trouble, and he's willing to sacrifice me to keep the peace."

Nell looked skeptical. "Is that the truth or some more of your malarkey?"

"Buckley ordered me not to leave town, and Denny just got through warning me to stick close to the Bella Union. That pretty well tells the tale, doesn't it?"

Starbuck was improvising now. By threading a strand of truth into the web of fabrication, he hoped to draw her over to his side. She was silent for a time, her face blank, her eyes opaque. Then, finally, she sighed and her expression softened.

"Okay, lover, I'm a sucker for a sob story and you've got me hooked. How can I help?"

"First off," Starbuck said quickly, "show me how to slip out of here without being seen—maybe later, some-time after we've gone to your room. That way Denny will think I'm tucked in for the night."

"Are you planning to skip Frisco?"

"No," Starbuck said without guile. "Buckley ordered me to come up with the hundred thousand by tomor-row. I've got it stashed somewhere safe, and I want to deliver it on my own. That'll show good faith, and go a long way toward getting me out of the middle."

"All right," Nell agreed. "Denny had a dumbwaiter installed to bring meals up to the third floor. Once the kitchen closes, we'll use that to get you downstairs and then you can slip out the alley door. What's next?"

"I want the story on Buckley, the whole ball of wax. If he decides to play rough, I'll need something to trade, something he'd consider worth a standoff."

"Holy Hannah," Nell said with a theatrical shudder. "You ask a lot, don't you?"

"Only enough to keep me alive."

"Don't kid yourself." Nell looked at him with dulled eyes. "Buckley doesn't have to bargain with anybody. He has a dozen different ways to silence you, and all of them permanent."

"A man plays the cards he's dealt. It's that or run, and I've never been one to turn tail. Besides, I don't like the way Danny and Fung sandbagged me."

"What the hell? It's your funeral."

"Not yet." Starbuck grinned. "You just give me the lowdown on Buckley, and I'll bluff him right out of his socks."

"There's not a lot to tell. I only know what I've heard when Denny goes on a toot and lets his tongue wag too much."

"How long has Buckley been top dog?"

"Long before my time. Twenty years, maybe more."

"Jesus," Starbuck marveled. "He must be tough. How'd he get his start?"

"The Tenderloin," Nell replied. "From what I gather, he killed the previous boss and just stepped into his shoes."

"You're saying a blind man was able to pull that off?"

"Well, he wasn't blind then. According to Denny, he

was wounded in the shootout and lost his sight afterward. His men stuck by him and he branched out from there."

"Why would they stick by a blind man?"

"Because he's one brainy bastard! Even without eyes, he can outthink lugheads like Denny. On top of that, he's masterminded every crooked deal in this town. Nothing moves without his say-so."

"Are you talking about Chinatown and the Coast?"

"No." Nell slowly shook her head. "I'm talking about Frisco, from the bay to the Golden Gate."

"Politics!" Starbuck's eyes narrowed with sudden comprehension. "That's what you meant earlier, wasn't it. When you said something about the second oldest profession?"

Nell bobbed her head. "Buckley *is* the Democratic Party. That's why Denny calls him Mr. Frisco. His wardheelers deliver the votes and he owns city hall like he'd foreclosed on the mortgage."

"So it's not fear—personal fear—that keeps Denny and Fung in line. They toe the mark because he's the political kingfish. Is that it?"

"No question about it," Nell affirmed. "He handpicked Denny to run the Coast, and the same with Fung in Chinatown. One word from him and they'd both be out on their ears. He made them and he can break them. It's just that simple."

"In other words," Starbuck mused thoughtfully, "Denny's plug-uglies and Fung's hatchet men couldn't save them no matter what."

"That's the setup," Nell remarked. "They've got the muscle, but Buckley's got the clout. He controls the mayor and the police department and every patronage job in the city. If he says Denny and Fung are out, then they're out. Period!"

Starbuck considered a moment. "How about pay-offs? The take on the Coast alone must be worth a fortune. Is there a bagman—a go-between—or does Denny deal directly with Buckley?"

"Search me." Nell gave Starbuck a bemused look. "I only know what I hear, and nobody talks about pay-offs. Even when he's drunk, Denny's not that thick."

"What about graft? Bribes? Anyone with Buckley's power has to knock down a mint with under-the-table loot."

"Oh, I imagine he robs the city like a bandit. But you couldn't prove it by me. I've never heard a rumor to that effect, much less read anything in the newspapers. He keeps a tight lid on the operation, real hush-hush. They way I get it, nobody but him knows the full score."

"How do you mean?"

"Well, it's like he wears two hats. One for politics and one for vice. He keeps them separate, never mixes one with the other. So nobody down here has any real pull with city hall or the police department. It all begins and ends with Buckley."

"Very cagey," Starbuck nodded. "One king with two kingdoms. Nobody trusts anyone else, so there's never a chance they'll join forces and kick him off the throne."

"I told you he's a brainy bastard."

"All the more reason for me to show up with the money tomorrow."

Nell smiled wanly. "You'd better think about to-night, lover. Otherwise, there won't be any tomorrow."

"As a matter of fact"—Starbuck leaned forward and poured the last of the champagne—"we're going to order another bottle of bubbly and pretend we're having ourselves a high old time. When we start up to your room, I want Denny to think we're sloshed to the gills.

That way he won't get any funny notions and come tip-toeing around in the night."

"What about when we get to the room?"

"What about it?"

"Do we have to pretend then," Nell vamped him with a sultry look, "or can we play it for real?"

Starbuck laughed. "We'll play it any whichaway you like. How's that sound?"

"Love it!" Neil giggled and clapped her hands. "Simply love it, Mr. Lovett."

Starbuck wasn't sure whether she intended a pun. Nor was he curious enough to pursue it further. His thoughts turned instead to the dumbwaiter and the long night ahead.

Dawn suddenly seemed all too close for comfort.

Chapter Twelve

She had the gift of natural repose, not unlike a sleeping cat. She lay curled in the iron band of his arm, cloyed with the scent of love. Her breasts dipped and swelled with the rise and fall of his breathing.

Their lovemaking had been slow and tender. Tonight she had given herself completely, and he had brought her to full and wondrous climax. Her undulations timed to the questing thrust of his manhood, they joined in an explosive burst of sweet agony. In that final moment, her contractions had held him fast, draining him, and she discovered something she had known with no other man. She found enkindled need, and the stirring of emotion.

Now, awake and restive, Starbuck's thoughts centered on more practical matters. One step remained before they parted for the night. She had committed herself by talking openly and agreeing to assist in his escape from the Bella Union. Yet he distrusted any arrangement based solely on emotion; troublesome second thoughts might later cause her to regret the act. He felt the need to further guarantee her switch of allegiance from O'Brien. Loyalty, in his experience, was determined only in part by the degree of jeopardy one person was willing to risk for another. The greater part of loyalty was anchored to self-interest, and he saw that as an essential element yet to be realized. He wanted her obligated not to him but to herself. A commitment whereby she would lose greatly in the event she was tempted to backslide.

Starbuck patted her on the rump and gently disengaged from her close embrace. Then he stretched, yawning, and swung his legs over the side of the bed.

"Time to get a move on."

"I know, damnit." Nell sat up in bed, her breasts round and firm in the dim light. "Why is it the good things never last?"

Her words presented an opening, and Starbuck seized on the opportunity. "Funny you mentioned that. I've been lying there thinking the same thing myself."

"You have?"

"Well, not exactly the way you mean, but pretty close. I got to toying with an idea about the future."

"Whose future?"

"Yours and mine."

"Honestly?" Nell said on an indrawn breath. "You really mean it?"

"Honest Injun." Starbuck gathered his pants off a nearby chair and began dressing. "Course, it all depends on how things turn out with Buckley."

"All what?"

"Nothing's certain, but let's play 'suppose' a minute. Suppose Buckley puts his stamp of approval on the deal. Suppose Denny and Fung salute and figure they'd be wiser to obey orders, and I end up with my hundred virgins. Suppose I take the girls back to Colorado and open a string of cathouses. In other words, suppose it all works out just the way I'd planned."

"I'll bite," Nell said, thoroughly mystified. "Suppose it does?"

"Then I'll need someone to run the operation for me. Someone like you."

"Me!" Nell squealed. "You're not serious?"

"The hell I'm not!" Starbuck began stuffing his shirt-tail into his pants, and gave her a dopey grin. "I've got big ideas and plenty of money, but I'm sort of shy on know-how. You said it yourself, when you asked me if I'd ever run a whorehouse. I guess that's what put the notion in my head."

"There's not all that much to it, not really."

"Say's you." Starbuck screwed up his face in a frown. "I don't know beans from buckshot about anything. One house would be headache enough for a tyro like me. But I aim to open four houses all at once! Think on that a minute."

"You're right," Nell conceded. "An operation that size could cause you some grief."

"Grief!" Starbuck snorted. "Christ, I'd be worse off than a one-legged man in a kicking contest. Just for openers, I'd have to hire a madam for each house. Then I'd have to figure out a way to keep them honest and make goddamn sure their books are straight. Otherwise, they could skim off the cream and leave me wondering how I went broke so fast."

"Honey, I hate to be the one to tell you, but the madams aren't your real problem. It's the girls! When you put that many females under one roof, it turns into a slam-bang catfight, night and day. Once you lose control, the whole operation could go to hell in a handbasket."

"That's my point," Starbuck said forcefully. "I need

someone to select the right madams and ride herd on all five houses. A supervisor or manager, someone who knows all the tricks of the trade. To my way of thinking, that someone is you."

"You really mean it, don't you?"

"Damn right!" Starbuck sensed it was time to dangle the carrot. "Matter of fact, I've already thought it out, and I'm willing to offer you ten percent right off the top. With four houses, I figure we'll rake in an easy million a year, maybe more. Your slice wouldn't exactly be termed chicken feed."

"Omigawd!" Nell whispered, awestruck. "A hundred thousand dollars! I'd be rich!"

"The sky's the limit," Starbuck observed grandly. "We'd make a helluva team, you and me. No telling where it would end."

Nell's head was buzzing. She suddenly saw an opportunity to put the Bella Union and the Barbary Coast behind her. The manager of a Colorado whorehouse empire was by no means a candidate for sainthood. Still, it was the only profession she knew, and it was several rungs up the ladder from the life she'd led in Frisco. Moreover, it offered the chance for financial independence, wealth beyond anything she had ever imagined. Which meant never again having to spread her legs for whiskey-soaked highrollers and pot-gutted old men.

Then there was Harry Lovett. He evoked responses in her that were all but forgotten. A sense of tenderness and affection, the deep-felt exhilaration of needing and being needed. On the surface he was glib and conniving, a grifter out to make his mark and devil take the hindmost. Yet there were quicksilver splinters of time in which she'd caught fleeting glimpses of the man beneath the rough exterior. A sensitive man with wit and understanding, even a trace of compassion. Knowing all that, she too wondered where it might end. Other whores had married their way out of the houses, so the idea was by no means farfetched. Harry Lovett might very well be the man for her. A chance for a fresh start and a new life. Her last chance.

At length, dizzied by the thought, she realized he was waiting on an answer. Then, on the verge of replying, a shadow of anxiety clouded her features. She suddenly remembered who she was and where she was. The star whore of the Bella Union, and no less a prisoner than the slave girls of Chinatown. Denny O'Brien always collected on a debt, and she owed him . . . more than she cared to admit.

"I'm sorry, Harry." She smiled the saddest smile he'd ever seen, and shook her head. "It's a great idea, but it wouldn't work."

"Why the hell not?"

"Nobody quits Denny," she said simply. "It's a rule of the house, and he doesn't make exceptions. Especially in my case."

"Forget O'Brien," Starbuck countered. "Once Buckley gives the go-ahead, we're off and running."

"I don't understand."

"Nothing to it," Starbuck scoffed. "I'll tell Buckley that either you're included in the package or it queers the whole deal."

"Suppose he calls your bluff?"

"Not a chance in a thousand. Fung would go off like a skyrocket and accuse O'Brien of deliberately scuttling the deal. That'd give Buckley more troubles than he's got now. He just wouldn't stand for it."

"You sound awful sure of yourself."

"Why not?" Starbuck laughed. "Once I make up my mind to something, that's it! Either I get you in the bargain or the deal's off. I'll just buy myself some whores from somebody else."

"You'd do that for me?"

"Hide and watch. One way or another, you're on your way to Colorado."

Nell bounded out of bed and threw herself on him. She smothered him with kisses, her arms circled around his neck, and finally planted one soundly on his mouth. When he pried her loose, her face was lighted with an exhuberant childlike glow.

"I hope that doesn't wear off before we get to Colorado."

"Honeybun, you haven't seen anything yet. Wait till I really get warmed up!"

"Tell you what I do see." Starbuck looked her up and down. "You step out in the hall like that and we're liable to draw a crowd."

Nell laughed a bawdy little laugh. Then she turned, wigwagging her fanny, and jiggled to the wardrobe. She slipped into a housecoat and began buttoning it up. All the while, she was humming softly under her breath.

Watching her, Starbuck wasn't proud of himself. Exactly as he'd planned, he had spoon-fed her a fairy tale and she had swallowed it whole. She was now in his camp, and there was virtually no chance she would betray him to O'Brien. Yet, however much her loyalty was tested, she would come out on the short end of the stick. Her days on the Barbary Coast were numbered, and from tonight onward the future itself would prove highly uncertain. Not for the first time, it occurred to him that the detective business was a dirty game. He felt somehow soiled by what he'd done. All the more so because he'd done it before and would very likely do it again.

"I'm ready anytime you are, lover."

Starbuck nodded, watching her a moment longer. "Any idea what you'll tell O'Brien in the morning?"

"Why, I'll just bat my baby-blues and tell him you slipped out while I was asleep. He'll never know the difference."

Starbuck smiled. "You know something? You would've made a helluva con man."

"Honey, a whore spends her whole life on the con."

She laughed softly and led the way to the door. After a quick peek outside, she signaled the all-clear. Then they stepped into the hall and walked toward the dumbwaiter.

A light fog hung over the city like gossamer curtains. Starbuck stopped at the entrance to the alleyway and checked the street in both directions. The hour was late, and he saw no one but a gang of drunken sailors weaving toward the waterfront. He crossed the street and strode off in the direction of the Palace Hotel.

The fog was an unexpected ally. Streetlamps, shrouded in a fuzzy glow, were visible half a block away. But the lampposts themselves were hidden by the swirling gray mist. He thought it unlikely that anyone could trail him in such weather. Still, all things considered, too much vigilance was better than too little. At the corner of Sutter and Montgomery, he stepped quickly into the darkened doorway of an office building. Waiting several moments, he listened intently, alert for the sound of footsteps. He heard nothing, and there were no signs of movement near the intersection. Presently, satisfied he wasn't being followed, he left the doorway and turned the corner. He reversed directions and disappeared into the fog. He walked swiftly toward Nob Hill.

Some ten minutes later, a bleary-eyed servant admitted him to the mansion of Charles Crocker. He was ushered into the study and asked to wait. Embers still simmered in the fireplace, and he soon rekindled a cheery blaze. Standing with his back to the fire, he warmed himself, slowly inspecting the room. The wooden panels were polished walnut, and one entire wall was bookshelves, stuffed from floor to ceiling with tomes bound in Moroccan leather. The books appeared untouched by human hands, and, quite probably, unread. He was examining a framed Audubon etching when the study door opened.

Charles Crocker marched into the room and slammed the door with a resounding thud. His eyes were gummed with sleep and he looked even fatter attired in a nightshirt and woolen robe. His expression was one of acute annoyance.

"What the hell do you mean coming here at this hour? Don't you realize it's after four o'clock?"

Starbuck returned his stare with sardonic amusement. "Crooks don't keep civilized hours. I operate on their timetable these days."

"Well, it better be important." Crocker flopped down in an overstuffed armchair. "I'm not accustomed to being awakened in the middle of the night."

"It's important." Starbuck took a chair across from him, lit a cigar. "Are you familiar with a man named Christopher Buckley?"

Crocker gave him a look of walleyed amazement. "Whether I am or not has no bearing on our business. Why do you ask?"

"Because he's the man behind your train robbers."

"You're out of your mind!"

"Think so?" Starbuck blew a plume of smoke into the air. "Suppose I fill you in on the last few days. Then you can decide for yourself."

Crocker groaned and slumped deeper into his chair. Starbuck briefly outlined everything he'd uncovered since their last meeting. He established the link between the train robbers and Denny O'Brien, then went on to describe the deal he'd struck with Fung Jing Toy. From there, he recounted the conversation with Buckley and the gist of the problems entailed. He omitted few details, and firmly demonstrated the chain of command in San Francisco's underworld. His report ended with a summary of his arrangement with Buckley. He stressed the time element and the need for speed.

"So that's it," he concluded. "To pull it off, I'll have to produce the hundred thousand no later than noon today."

A thick silence settled over the room. Crocker, obviously disgruntled, gazed at Starbuck for a long, speculative moment. Then he shook his head in stern disapproval.

"I'm afraid you've overstepped the bounds of your assignment. I retained you to catch a band of train robbers, not organize a civic crusade. Your zeal is to be commended, Mr. Starbuck. But my only interest is in halting the robberies, nothing more."

"Why settle for half a loaf?" Starbuck gave him a hard, wise look. "We can capture Red Ned Adair, then offer him immunity to turn state's evidence against O'Brien. After that, we take it step by step, playing them off one against the other. When we're through, we'll have Buckley and most of his stooges behind bars. It's a perfect setup, made to order."

"No, thank you," Crocker said with an unpleasant grunt. "Your instructions are to eliminate Adair and his gang of robbers. The assignment begins and ends there. Do I make myself clear?"

All at once the truth came home to Starbuck. A practicing cynic, and something of an iconoclast, he had always viewed the world as a place of dupes and rogues. The dupes, in the natural course of things, were preyed upon by the rogues. Yet, in his absorption with the case, he'd forgotten that Charles Crocker, one of the great robber barons of the era, was essentially a rogue. Since rogues seldom locked horns with other rogues, Crocker quite naturally had no interest in exposing Christopher Buckley. The premise gained even more credence when politics were involved. A can of worms, once opened, might lead anywhere. Perhaps to the Central Pacific, and Charles Crocker himself.

"Here's the deal," Starbuck said stonily. "You have the money delivered to my hotel room before noon. I'll follow the plan I've just laid out and push it to the limit." He paused, took a long draw on his cigar. "Now, maybe you don't like the idea, but you'd like the alternative even less. Turn me down and I'll take the story to the newspapers. I've got a hunch your name would end up in big, bold headlines."

"Confound you!" Crocker's eyes were angry, reproachful. "I won't be dictated to, and I damn well won't allow you to bullyrag me. Take heed, Mr. Starbuck!"

"Save your breath," Starbuck said with a clenched smile. "When I accepted the assignment, I told you how I work. I don't take orders and I don't quit till the job's done. Buckley's a spoiler, the worst kind, and I figure he deserves to get axed. One way or another, I aim to see that it happens."

Crocker's features colored dark with blood. He rose and moved to the fireplace. Hands clasped behind his back, he stood for a long time staring into the flames. At last, he took a deep breath, blew it out heavily.

When he turned around, his face was pale and there was a look of resignation in his eyes.

"Very well," he murmured in assent. "I'll go along with your request. But I warn you, Mr. Starbuck. Under no circumstances is my name to be connected with Christopher Buckley! Defy me on that and I will personally hound you out of the detective business."

"Why, hell's fire!" Starbuck laughed, a sudden harsh sound in the still room. "You just leave it to me, Mr. Crocker. I'll make you a hero! Goddamn if I won't."

"Yes, I agree." Crocker nodded gravely. "You are truly damned if you don't, Mr. Starbuck."

"Aren't we all?" Starbuck said with a cynical grin. "Have a seat, and let me tell you what I've got in mind."

Crocker walked to his chair and sat down. His expression was solemn and his mood attentive. Starbuck waited a moment, puffing quietly on his cigar. Then, with obvious relish, he began talking.

The first step, he explained, was the capture of Red Ned Adair.

Chapter Thirteen

Shortly before dawn, two days later, Starbuck left the Palace Hotel by a side entrance. Once outside, he crossed the street and ducked into an alleyway. He waited several moments, until he was certain he wasn't being tailed. Then he turned and walked swiftly toward the Central Pacific train yard.

All the preparations necessary to his plan had been completed. Yesterday, at the stroke of noon, a package had been delivered to his hotel room. Inside were several packets of bills, large-denomination notes totaling $100,000, and a terse message from Charles Crocker. According to instructions, Crocker had quietly issued two orders. The first concerned today's morning train to Los Angeles: there were to be no extra guards on the express car. Crocker had announced the measure as a new gambit to deceive the robbers into believing there was nothing of value in today's shipment. At the same time, he directed that a major transfer from the San Francisco mint be put aboard the train. Starbuck had every confidence that the gang's inside man—the Judas

—would leak word of this unusual operation. Red Ned Adair was virtually certain to rob the morning southbound.

Crocker's second order had been carried out in absolute secrecy. A trusted aide, less than an hour ago, had awakened Captain Tom Kelly, Chief of Security for the Central Pacific. The aide, under firm instructions never to leave Kelly's side, had then accompanied the security chief while he routed seven express guards from their beds. The men were quickly collected in the chill predawn darkness and bundled aboard waiting carriages. Once assembled, they were driven to a warehouse on the edge of the Central Pacific train yard. There, they were issued rifles and sidearms, then told to wait. Kelly's instructions, delivered by the aide, were specific and purposely vague. A man named Starbuck would arrive at the warehouse shortly before sunrise. All details regarding the mission would be explained at that time. Kelly was to follow his orders explicitly and without question.

Hurrying toward the train yard, Starbuck was satisfied that everything was now in place. Yesterday afternoon, following a meeting with Buckley, he had deposited the $100,000 in a bank selected by the political kingpin. The ploy, much as he'd expected, bought him time and got Denny O'Brien out of his hair. Within the hour, the second phase of his plan would swing into operation. Accompanied by the security force, he would travel southward from the city. Not long after their departure, the morning train, with an unguarded express car, would roll toward Los Angeles. The bait was laid and the trap would be sprung somewhere around noontime. All that remained was to ambush Red Ned Adair.

A few minutes before dawn, Starbuck stepped through the door of the warehouse. A group of men, jammed together in a stench of sweating bodies, were gathered around a potbellied stove. Their faces were grim, and most of them, still half-asleep, were holding steaming mugs of coffee. Conversation stopped, replaced by watchful silence, as he closed the door and moved forward. The only sound was a coffeepot, hissing and rattling on top the stove.

Starbuck, approaching closer, sensed the tension. Yet nothing in his tone or manner revealed the slightest trace of concern. He spoke with authority, iron sureness.

"Captain Kelly?"

"That's me."

A man of formidable size, tall and massively built, separated from the group. His hands were large and gnarled, and his voice was a stilled rumble. There was a heavy-lidded, lizard-like alertness to his eyes.

"I'm Luke Starbuck."

Kelly accepted his handshake, frowning. "Pleased to meet you."

"Has anyone left this room since you were brought here?"

"No," Kelly acknowledged stiffly. "We've not been here more than a few minutes ourselves."

"Good," Starbuck nodded. "Ask your men to finish their coffee and get ready to go."

"Go where?" Kelly raised an uncertain eyebrow. "I was given to understand you'd fill us in on the particulars."

"I will," Starbuck said evenly, "when the time's right."

Kelly's eyes became veiled. "Well, now, maybe you wouldn't mind explaining what all the mystery's about. We're more than a little curious, as you might well appreciate."

"Sorry," Starbuck said with an odd smile. "Where

we're going—and what we've been assigned to do—will have to wait till we get there."

"Is that so?" Kelly demanded churlishly. "Then maybe you could at least tell us why we were rousted out in the middle of the night? Without so much as a by-your-leave!"

Starbuck gave him a swift, appraising glance. "Captain Kelly, you've got your orders and I've got mine. Suppose we let it go at that and get on with the job?"

"By the sweet Jesus!" Kelly said loudly. "I'm responsible for these men, and I'll not take them off to God knows where until I've had an explanation."

"For the moment, you've had all the explanation you need. We're on official business, and at the proper time, I'll lay it out for you in black and white. That's twice I've said it, so don't make me repeat myself again."

"Oh, repeat yourself, is it?" Kelly said with a sudden glare. "Well, mister-whoever-the-hell-you-are, I don't know you from Paddy's pig! You could talk yourself blue in the face and I'll not move from this spot unless I hear the reason why."

A vague disquiet settled over Starbuck. Something told him there was more to Kelly's objections than met the eye. Aside from resentment, which was natural enough at being reduced to second-in-command, there was some darker element just below the surface. The man was too antagonistic, too intractable, far more so than the situation dictated. Yet Starbuck hadn't the time nor the inclination to pursue it further. Sunrise was the deadline for their departure, and faint shafts of light were already streaming through the windows. He decided to force the issue.

"Captain Kelly," he said flatly, "the only thing you need to know is that I speak for Charles Crocker. Your instructions were to follow my orders to the letter. If that puts your nose out of joint, that's your problem. Take it up with Crocker when we get back."

"Instructions!" Kelly roared. "I've had no instructions, except from Crocker's flunky. Considering your high-handed manner, that won't do. Not for Tom Kelly, it won't!"

"Like it or lump it," Starbuck said roughly. "You're under my oders, and that's that."

"Says you." Kelly's nostrils flared. "I'll just have myself a talk with Crocker and see who's giving the orders around here. I've a strong notion there's a nigger-in-the-woodpile somewhere."

Starbuck fixed him with a pale stare. "I can't allow that."

"Blood of Christ!" Kelly said furiously. "I wasn't asking your permission. You can go or stay as you please! I mean to have a word with Charlie Crocker."

"No." Starbuck's face took on a hard cast. "You're not going anywhere except where I tell you to go."

"Out of my way!"

Kelly brushed past him and started toward the door. Starbuck struck out in a shadowy movement. He buried his fist in the big man's kidney, and Kelly's mouth opened in a great whoosh of breath. Shifting slightly, Starbuck spun him around and exploded two splintering punches flush on the jaw. Kelly went down like a pole-axed steer. He lay still a moment, then groaned and rolled heavily to his knees. He tried to rise, but his face twisted in a grimace of pain and he remained kneeling. Starbuck, scarcely winded, stood over him.

"Enough?"

"Enough," Kelly bobbed his head. "I think you busted something inside."

"You'll live."

There was a gruff buzz from the other men, and Starbuck turned. His brow seamed, and he eyed them with a steady, uncompromising gaze. When he spoke, his voice was scratchy, abrasive.

"Only one man gives the orders, and that's me. Anybody sees it otherwise, now's the time to step forward."

No one stepped forward. He waited several moments, then turned once more to face Kelly. The big man climbed slowly to his feet, and stood with a hand clutched tightly to his kidney. Starbuck gestured toward the door.

"I want everybody outside and in those carriages . . . now."

Kelly looked dazed, punchy. He stared down at the floor, tightlipped, his teeth locked against the pain. At length, he drew a deep breath and glanced up at his men.

"Let's go," he rasped hoarsely. "Everybody in the carriages."

Starbuck led the way through the door. Outside, he split the men into two groups, indicating Kelly was to ride in the lead carriage. When everyone was settled, he climbed aboard and took a seat beside the security chief. He ordered the driver to head south, and as they rolled out of the train yard the sky lightened into perfect cloudless blue. He glanced back and a slow smile creased his mouth.

The morning train stood chuffing smoke outside the terminal.

A mile or so north of the farmhouse Starbuck ordered the carriages off the road. Several hundred yards to the east, the wooded creek meandered southward.

Following his directions, the carriages were driven across a grassy field and halted beneath the trees.

There he left Kelly and the men, and struck off on foot downcreek. His recollection of the gang's hideout was fairly accurate. Still, some time had passed since he'd trailed Adair and the band of robbers to the farmhouse. Leaving nothing to chance, he thought it wiser to personally scout the terrain. Today there was no margin for error.

Some while later he spotted the farmhouse through the trees. Quiet as a drifting hawk, he approached to within fifty yards, then went belly down on the ground. He crawled forward and stopped under the shelterbelt of woods. Hidden by shadow, he removed his hat and slowly scanned the layout.

Off to one side of the house, the woman was hanging a wash on a clothesline. Her husband was puttering around in a shed near the barn. The corral stood empty and the barn doors were closed. All of which confirmed his judgment about Red Ned Adair. The gang had ridden out earlier on the saddlehorses, leaving their carriages concealed in the barn. The holdup, in all likelihood, had already occurred. Without extra guards, the Central Pacific southbound was a pushover, and the express-car messenger would have offered only token resistance. Even now, the robbers were probably following the same twisting route back to the farmhouse.

Starbuck turned and studied the high ground across the creek. From the top of the knoll, he recalled, there was a clear view of the farmhouse and the barn and the fields beyond. Outlaws were creatures of habit, and he thought it reasonable to assume they would again approach the hideout by way of the wooded knoll. The time to strike was when they dismounted outside the corral. Flushed with success, saddlebags stuffed with loot, their defenses would be at a low ebb. Further, with the barn doors closed, they would be caught in the open with nowhere to run. All that, combined with the element of surprise, should turn the trick very nicely. Barring mishap, the robbers would never know what hit them.

Worming back to the creek, Starbuck rose and took off at a dogtrot upstream. Several minutes later he reached the carriages and found the men sprawled on the ground, smoking and talking quietly amongst themselves. Kelly stood off to one side, propped against the base of a tree. His expression was sullen and withdrawn.

The men scrambled to their feet as Starbuck halted near the lead carriage. He signaled them to gather around and waited while Kelly ambled over to join the group. Then he went straight to the point.

"You're all aware of the train holdups that have taken place over the past year. I was hired by the Central Pacific to catch the robbers, and I've located their hideout. It's a farmhouse, about a mile downstream, on the west side of the creek. Today, we're going to lay an ambush and put an end to those holdups."

A murmur of excitement swept over the men. Starbuck hesitated a moment, then silenced them with upraised palms. "Here's the way it'll work. Once we get downstream, I'll assign you to positions and point out the best fields of fire. Then we wait till the gang rides in and dismounts at the corral. That's when we hit 'em."

"A question." Kelly nailed him with a corrosive stare. "Who's their leader, and how many are there in the gang?"

"Glad you asked," Starbuck remarked. "Altogether, there'll be seven men. The leader's a gent by the name of Red Ned Adair. He's easy to spot because he's a carrot-head, bright red hair." He paused, glancing around the group. "Adair is not—I repeat—he is not to be killed. I want him taken alive."

"Are you saying," Kelly asked bluntly, "that you want the others killed?"

"When you shoot a man," Starbuck replied calmly, "I've always found it's best to kill him. Otherwise, you're liable to make him mad and then he'll kill you."

Kelly gave him a long, searching stare. "What about this fellow Adair? He'll more than likely be shooting back at us. Are you saying we're not to return his fire?"

"Nobody," Starbuck underscored the word with heavy emphasis, "will fire at Adair but me. I'll either cripple him or keep him pinned down till the fight's over. So if you catch red hair in your sights, shift to another target. That's a direct order."

Kelly offered an elaborate shrug and said no more. The other men obediently bobbed their heads in affirmation. When there were no further questions, Starbuck dropped to one knee on the ground. He took a twig and sketched a crude map in the dirt.

"Here's the lay of the land. We'll go downstream and then . . ."

A brassy noonday sun stood high overhead. Squatted behind a tree, Starbuck watched as Red Ned Adair led his gang down the knoll and forded the creek. The robbers were laughing and exchanging wisecracks, clearly in high spirits. The holdup, quite obviously, had come off without a hitch.

Standing, Starbuck quickly surveyed the wooded terrain. Kelly and four men were posted across the stream, on the forward slope of the knoll. Concealed by undergrowth, they were all but invisible beneath the dim shadows of the trees. The three remaining guards were flanked directly to his right, spread out along the west bank of the creek. He had assigned himself the point position, nearest the farmhouse. His shot would be the signal to open fire.

Easing around, he took a quick peek from behind the tree. The gang was aproaching the corral, and the farmer walked forward to greet them. The woman, standing at the corner of the house, looked on in silence. He thumbed the hammer on his carbine and wedged the butt into the hollow of his shoulder. He centered the sights on Red Ned Adair.

A shot cracked and bark exploded beside his head.

Cursing savagely, he crouched and swung around as the gunfire became general. His gaze went across the creek and he saw Kelly jacking another shell into his own carbine. Without thought, operating on sheer instinct, he caught the security chief's chest in his sights and levered three quick shots. The slugs jolted Kelly backward a step at a time. The last one slammed into his brisket, splattering bone and gore, and he dropped the carbine. His hands splayed and clawed at empty air, then his legs buckled. He hit the ground and went tumbling head over heels down the knoll.

Starbuck whirled even before the body rolled to a halt. All around him the guards' rifles continued to bark, laying down a heavy volume of fire. He stepped around the tree and saw that Red Ned Adair and three of the gang were still mounted. Their horses were spooked, pitching and rearing in wild gyrations. Yet their sixguns were out, and while their aim was none too good, they were blazing away at the treeline. A quick glance confirmed that the farmer and the other robbers were down, either dead or dying.

All in an instant, Starbuck realized his only chance was to drop Adair's horse. He stepped clear of the trees, looking for an opening, and advanced toward the corral. Behind him, a staccato volley of gunfire broke loose, and the last three gang members pitched from their saddles. He saw Adair look in his direction and sensed he'd been recognized. A split-second later the outlaw leader fired, and a slug snarled past overhead. Then, before he could align his sights, Adair got control of his horse and took off down the road at a gallop. He let go a snap shot, but knew he'd missed even as he pulled the trigger. Horse and rider vanished in the next moment, blocked from view by the house.

Starbuck sprinted toward the corral. The gunfire abruptly ceased and an eerie silence descended over the farm. From behind, he heard the guards shouting to one another and vaguely noted the sound of running footsteps. The outlaws' bodies, grotesque in death, littered the ground closer to the barn. He charged past them, only to spot Adair far in the distance. He swore, skidding to a stop, and flung the carbine in the dirt. Then, almost a reflex action, he turned and caught up the reins of a loose horse. He stepped into the saddle as the guards approached and slowed to a walk. His finger stabbed out at the man in the lead.

"You!" he ordered. "Arrest the woman in the house and charge her with accessory to robbery. Then take Kelly's body to Charles Crocker. Deliver it personally! Tell him it's a present from me."

The guard gawked at him. "A present?"

"You heard right," Starbuck growled. "A present named Judas."

"What about you, Mr. Starbuck? What'll I tell him about you?"

"Tell him to look for me when he sees me."

Starbuck reined sharply around and gigged the horse in the ribs. Some distance away he saw a plume of dust drifting upward against the muslin-blue sky. He rode toward San Francisco.

Chapter Fourteen

Late that afternoon, Denny O'Brien arrived at the Snug Café. After pounding on the alley door, he was admitted by a startled Chinese dishwasher. Knuckles Jackson, who doubled as one of Buckley's bodyguards, was hurriedly summoned from the front of the café.

O'Brien, whose manner was agitated and somewhat irrational, demanded to see Buckley. His appearance at the café during the daytime was unprecedented, and led to a heated argument. At last, albeit reluctantly, Jackson left him in the storeroom and went upstairs. Several moments passed; then the door opened and he Several moments passed, then the door opened and he son gave him a look reserved for fools and harebrained Irishmen.

Buckley was seated behind the desk. His composure was monumental, and his expression betrayed no hint of aggravation. Yet, when he spoke, his tone was clipped and stiff, angry.

"You were told never to come here in daylight."

"I'm sorry, but I had no choice."

"On the contrary, only an imbecile fails to exercise choice. Your presence indicates that you deliberately *chose* to ignore my wishes."

"For Chrissake, nobody saw me!"

"You miss the point," Buckley said with sudden wrath. "I will not allow anyone to override my orders." He took out a pocket watch, opened the lid, and deftly fingered the exposed hands. "Five-o-seven! Which means it will be dark in less than two hours. I presume that never occurred to you?"

"What I have to say wouldn't wait."

"Indeed?" Buckley returned the watch to his vest pocket. "Has the Bella Union burned down, or is it some lesser calamity?"

"Lots worse." O'Brien dropped into a chair before the desk. "We've got trouble! A shitpot full of trouble."

"Perhaps you could be a bit more specific?"

"It's Harry Lovett," O'Brien said, clearing his throat. "I just found out the son-of-a-bitch is a Pinkerton."

Buckley received the news with surpassing calmness. "What leads you to believe so?"

"Him and a squad of railroad bulls jumped Ned Adair and his boys this morning. Suckered them into a trap and blasted the whole gang straight to hell."

"Does that include Adair?"

"No," O'Brien said quickly. "Ned fought his way clear. It was nip and tuck, but he came through without a scratch."

"A pity," Buckley observed dryly. "Exactly what happened?"

"Ned and his boys robbed the morning train to Los Angeles. His inside man at Central Pacific—the chief security bull—told him there wouldn't be any guards on the express car. Sure enough, there weren't, and the holdup went off slick as a whistle."

"No guards," Buckley mused to himself. "Offhand, I'd think that would have alerted Adair. It seems patently obvious."

O'Brien spread his hands in a gesture of bafflement. "None of it makes any sense. Kelly—that's the security bull—hadn't never tipped him wrong before. But god-damn if Kelly don't show up at the farmhourse—"

"Farmhouse?"

"Yeah, a farmhouse south of town. Ned used it as a cover whenever he pulled a holdup."

"Go on."

"Well, like I said, Kelly was there. Ned says he fired the first shot, evidently at someone in his own party. Then all of a sudden, Kelly goes down and the next thing you know, Lovett pops out from behind a tree. Ned thinks Kelly tried to get Lovett, and instead, Lovett got him."

"Brilliant." Buckley invested the word with scorn. "Did Adair deduce all that by himself?"

"Ned's no dimwit," O'Brien said defensively. "The way it looks, Kelly got himself boxed in and couldn't get word to Ned. Then he tried to turn it around at the last minute, and ended up dead."

"Greater love hath no man," Buckley added with satiric mockery. "Perhaps we could move on to the part about Lovett."

O'Brien hunched forward in his chair. "Ned spotted him the second he stepped out of the trees. Lovett was trying to draw a bead on him, but Ned winged a shot and took off. All his men were down, so it would've been suicide to stick around any longer."

"He's quite certain it was Lovett? In the heat of the moment, he couldn't have been mistaken?"

"No mistake," O'Brien said dourly. "It was Lovett, all right. Ned swears to it."

Buckley considered the thought. "Then we can surmise that Lovett had already identified Adair as the gang leader. Working backward, we can assume that Adair led him to you, and quite recently too. That would explain Lovett's little charade over the past week."

O'Brien looked blank. "What's a charade?"

"A deception," Buckley replied with cold hauteur. "One specifically engineered and acted out for gullible louts like yourself. It would appear our Mr. Lovett is an undercover operative for the Central Pacific."

"That's what I said!" O'Brien blurted out. "The bastard's a Pinkerton!"

"Perhaps." Buckley examined the notion a moment. "Whether he is or isn't seems a moot question at this point. What concerns me most is that you and your merry band of train robbers led him directly to me."

"The hell it did!" O'Brien denied hotly. "It was Fung! Except for him, you wouldn't have never heard of Lovett."

"You have a short memory." Buckley's voice dropped. "Fung was suspicious of him from the start. You also forget that I've warned you repeatedly about train holdups. I believe my comment was to the effect that the return in no way justified the risk."

"What's train holdups got to do with Fung?"

"Everything," Buckley said gruffly. "All of it involves greed, your greed. I gave you the Barbary Coast, but you weren't satisfied with that. You had to have something extra, smalltime side deals. Train robbery was one, and introducing Lovett to Fung was another. So you see, it's all of a piece, Denny. Bluntly put, you're too greedy for your own good . . . or mine."

"Wait a minute!" O'Brien objected. "You're not

blaming me for this Lovett thing, are you? Jesus Christ, how was I to know he's a Pinkerton?"

"Again, the point eludes you." Buckley dismissed it with a brusque gesture. "Let's press on, shall we? At the moment we have a larger problem, and unless I'm mistaken, it has little to do with today's train robbery."

"Oh?" O'Brien appeared thoroughly confounded. "What problem's that?"

"Harry Lovett," Buckley told him. "If his primary target was Adair, then why did he concoct such an elaborate cover story? Why get involved with you or Fung? Why risk a hundred thousand dollars merely to gain my confidence?" He paused, reflective. "Something of an enigma, isn't it?"

"I give up," O'Brien said, attentive now. "Why?"

"Because Adair was only a means to an end. On balance, that seems the only logical conclusion. Lovett was after bigger game from the very start. Whether or not he suspected it would bring him to my door, we'll probably never know. What matters is that it did, and he capitalized on it quite cleverly. Quite cleverly, indeed."

"You think he's after you?"

"I think that's precisely what he's after."

"So what do we do now?"

"A good question."

Buckley placed his elbows on the arms of his chair, steepled his fingers. His eyes, shaded by the tinted glasses, appeared metallic, glittering yet dead. O'Brien had the strange sensation that behind those eyes was something inhuman, even demonic. An elemental force that fed itself on hate and power, and the bones of anyone who stood in its way. One thought led to another, and he dimly pondered where that left him. Then, suddenly, Buckley's voice jarred him back to the present.

"I'm afraid I have some bad news for you, Denny."

"What kind of bad news?"

"Ned Adair is expendable," Buckley said with chilling simplicity. "I want you to get rid of him . . . today."

"Kill him?" O'Brien gave him a murky look. "What the hell for?"

"For the best of reasons." Buckley permitted himself a grim smile. "Without Adair there's no link to you, and therefore no link to me. Lovett will be left with nothing but allegations. And as we all know, allegations aren't worth a dime a dozen."

O'Brien massaged his nose, thinking. He knew, though the message was left unstated, that Ned Adair was not the subject at issue. His own knowledge of Frisco's underworld, and how the operation was structured, posed a far graver threat to Buckley. One false step and he himself would end up at the bottom of the bay. Yet, like many Irishmen, he was cursed with an obdurate nature and a volatile temper. He also possessed loyalty to those he considered friends; betrayal for the sake of expediency was to him the greatest blasphemy. His code had little to do with common standards of decency, but it was nonetheless the code by which he lived. He never welched on a deal or gaffed a friend—and he never betrayed a trust.

"I won't do it," he said stoutly. "Ned's been with me since the old days, and I've no better friend in the world. I'd sooner kill my own mother."

"An admirable sentiment," Buckley said with wintry malice. "However, in this case, we have to concern ourselves with the practical solution. If Adair were caught, and persuaded to talk, then your arrest would be a virtual certainty." He stopped, slowly shook his

157

head. "You know I can't allow that to happen, don't you, Denny?"

"Ned won't talk," O'Brien protested. "He'd go to the gallows before he opened his mouth. As for me, I've never ratted in my life, and I've no intention to start now."

"Indeed?" Buckley's tone was icy. "Then let me put it to you this way, Denny. Are you willing to risk your neck to save Adair?"

"Look here," O'Brien said stubbornly. "Why kill Ned when there's a better way? I'll put him on a ship tonight and send him off to China. Christ, he'd be gone two years, maybe more! By then, this whole thing will've blown over and be long forgotten."

Buckley immediately thought of Fung. Once in China, Adair could be dispatched by Fung's associates with Oriental efficiency and a minimum of fuss. For the moment it would salve O'Brien's rebellious mood; later, if necessary, Fung would be delighted to dispatch the Irishman, as well. Overall, it seemed the perfect solution to an unwieldy problem.

"Very well," he conceded with a show of tolerance. "We'll strike a compromise. You put Adair aboard the first clipper bound for China. Not tomorrow or the next day, but tonight! Any delay in shipping him out and all bets are off. Fair enough?"

"Plenty fair," O'Brien agreed. "I'll handle it myself so there won't be any slipups. Before midnight, Ned will kiss Frisco goodbye, and that's a promise."

"Don't fail me," Buckley reminded him. "Otherwise, I'll be forced to call your marker. Adair or you, that's the proposition. Understood?"

"Understood," O'Brien said in a resigned voice. "One way or another, I'll have him on his way with the evening tide."

"I'm sure you will, Denny."

O'Brien looked into the dead eyes and an involuntary chill touched his backbone. Unless he delivered on the promise, there was no doubt the marker would be called. Either Ned Adair vanished tonight or his own life was forfeit. There was no third choice.

Nell sensed trouble when O'Brien hurried through the door of the Bella Union. He looked not just angry, but somehow shaken, unnerved. A moment later intuition turned to certainty. He brushed past High Spade McQueen without a word and rushed up the stairs. Something was seriously wrong, and the source of the problem was hardly in question. Somehow it involved Red Ned Adair.

Earlier that afternoon, on her way downstairs, she'd seen Ned Adair enter O'Brien's suite. Covered with sweat and grime, he had left the impression that the Devil himself was on his heels. Before she reached the stairwell, O'Brien had erupted in a burst of profanity. The sound of his curses carried clearly along the hall, and she'd thought at the time that Adair had finally pulled one boner too many. Then, dismissing it from mind, she had gone on about her business.

Now, watching O'Brien take the stairs two at a time, she was struck by a wayward thought. She wondered if it somehow involved Harry Lovett. He hadn't put in an appearance last night, and she'd heard nothing from him today. That seemed to her very strange, out of character. Knowing she expected him, he was too considerate not to have sent a message. Unless he was unable to send a message!

Stranger still was the fact that Ned Adair hadn't set foot out of O'Brien's suite since arriving. Try as she might, she couldn't imagine a connection between Adair and Harry Lovett. Yet she was no great believer in coincidence. Adair was hiding from something or somebody, and whatever he'd done, it had thrown O'Brien into a towering rage. Added to Harry Lovett's curious disappearance, it seemed altogether too timely for mere coincidence. She suddenly decided to do a little eavesdropping.

A glance toward the barroom confirmed that McQueen's attention was diverted elsewhere. She casually mounted the stairs and made her way to the third floor. As she passed O'Brien's suite, which was next to her own room, she heard loud voices from inside. Quietly, she entered her room and went directly to the washstand. Long ago, she had discovered that the wall separating her quarters from O'Brien's was wafer-thin clapboard. Further, she'd found that a girl could easily get an earful, and learn all sorts of secrets. All it required was a water glass.

She placed the open end of the glass flush against the wall. Then she pressed her right ear tightly to the bottom of the glass, and stuck her finger in her left ear. The effect was not unlike that produced by a megaphone. Sounds were amplified, and voices carried with remarkable clarity. She listened closely, and the wall seemed to evaporate. An argument was raging, and in her mind's eye, it was not difficult to imagine their faces.

"I won't go! I don't give a shit what Buckley says. I won't go, and that's that!"

Ned Adair stopped pacing, suddenly turned and glared at O'Brien. Dull despair was etched on his features, and dark bruised-looking rings circled his eyes. He sat down heavily on a sofa, his face doughy and stunned. His stomach rolled, and an unmanning sense of nausea seized him. He shook his head wildly.

"Mexico, maybe." He passed a hand across his eyes and swallowed hard. "But I'll be goddamned if I'll go to China. Not me!"

"You're damned if you don't." O'Brien's voice was firm. "Unless you sail tonight, you're a dead man. No two ways about it, Ned."

"I'll take my chances," Adair said morosely. "All I need's a fast horse and an hour's head start. Buckley wouldn't never find me! Not in a million years."

"No soap," O'Brien informed him. "I gave my word to Buckley. You take off running and it's my neck that'll get chopped. I'd have to stop you—and I would."

Adair's jaw fell open, as though hinged. "Jesus, Mary and Joseph! Are you saying you'd kill me, Denny?"

O'Brien shrugged. "I'm saying I won't die for you. Now that you've brought the Pinkertons down on us, there's no way around it. You either sail for China or you get deep-sixed."

"You—" Adair stammered. "You're blaming me? It was you that opened the door to Lovett and took him under wing. I had nothing to do with it. Nothing!"

"No more of your guff!" O'Brien suddenly bellowed. "You're the one that robbed the train, and you're the one that led Lovett straight to the Bella Union. And to me, too! So dry up and take your medicine like a man. That's my final word on it, Ned."

Adair blinked several times. Under O'Brien's ugly stare, all his courage abruptly deserted him. He gloomily bowed his head and nodded. "Have it your way, Denny. I'd sooner sail the China Sea the rest of my life than have you down on me."

"That's the spirit!" O'Brien laughed heartily. "We'll sneak you down to Mother Bronson's joint after dark, and she'll arrange passage on the finest clipper in port.

Hell, it'll be like an ocean voyage, Ned! You'll have yourself a grand time."

Adair mumbled an inaudible reply. His eyes, oddly vacant, were fixed on the floor.

On the other side of the wall, Nell numbly lowered the water glass. She paled and her cheek muscles grew taut, and her face was no longer a pleasant sight. She felt swept up in a nightmare, the floodgates of fear suddenly opened and swirling madly about her. She crossed the room in a daze and sat down on the edge of the bed. Her ears rang with the words and she choked off a cry. She couldn't believe it, wouldn't believe it.

Harry Lovett a Pinkerton? Adair and O'Brien—even the blind man!—panicked by the dapper grifter who had shared her bed. The same devil-may-care jokester who had offered her a job and promised her a new life and sworn to take her away from the Barbary Coast. It wasn't true, none of it. For if it was, then he had lied to her, used her. She couldn't credit that, not from Harry Lovett.

Her head pulsated like a huge festering wound. She heard again the words of Denny O'Brien and she reasoned muzzily that it was a mistake. Some monstrous and terrifying mistake. She wondered what to do, and even as she asked herself the question, she knew she would do nothing. A girl had to live, and only a fool took sides when men drew the line.

She would wait and see, and do what she'd always done. She would go with the winner.

Chapter Fifteen

Nell looked wretched when she opened the door. Ugly lines strained her face and her features were smudged downward. She stared at him with a mixture of dismay and surprise, momentarily dumbstruck.

With a last glance along the hall, Starbuck stepped into her room and closed the door. He twisted the key, locking the door, then turned toward her. As though expecting applause, he doffed his hat and flashed his gold tooth in a wide grin. Her face blanched, eyes round as saucers.

"How did you get in here?"

Starbuck chuckled. "I bribed the cook to send me up in the dumbwaiter."

"The cook!" she repeated sharply. "Are you crazy?"

"Like a fox," Starbuck said with a jocular wink. "I told him we had a little hanky-panky going on the side. He took to the idea right away, even wished me luck. I got the feeling he's one of your secret admirers."

"You fool!" Her voice rose suddenly. "He'll report

it to McQueen. He's probably on his way out front right now."

"No chance," Starbuck assured her. "I slipped him a hundred, and told him there'd be another hundred when I come back down."

"What's to stop him from squealing to McQueen, then? Or weren't you worried about what happens to me when you leave?"

"Don't trouble yourself," Starbuck said lightly. "Silence goes to the highest bidder. I'll give him an extra hundred just to make sure he stays bought."

Nell regarded him with an odd steadfast look. "The way you bought me?"

"Bought you?" Starbuck saw anger, resentment, and a trace of fear in her eyes. "I don't get your meaning."

"The hell you don't!" she said furiously. "You're a lowdown rotten bastard, Harry Lovett! You promised me the moon and I went for it like a schoolgirl with a case of the vapors."

"What in Christ's name are you talking about?"

"You're a Pinkerton!" she said loudly, staring at him through a prism of tears. "A lying, good-for-nothing snake in the grass! I know the whole story, so don't try to deny it."

"A Pinkerton?" Starbuck was genuinely astounded. "Where the deuce did you get an idea like that?"

"From Denny." She sniffed and dabbed at the tears. "I overheard him talking to Ned Adair. I know you're after Ned for robbing trains and I know—"

"Slow down," Starbuck broke in quickly. "Ned Adair's here? He's somewhere in the Bella Union?"

She motioned toward the window. "You're too late," she said, indicating the deepening indigo of nightfall. "Denny took him—got him out of here—right after it turned dark."

"You started to say O'Brien took him somewhere, didn't you?"

She tossed her head. "Wouldn't you like to know?"

"I have to know," Starbuck said urgently. "It's important, Nell. So damned important you wouldn't believe it."

"Tough tit, hotshot!" She made an agitated gesture with both hands. "I don't talk to Pinkertons."

"I'm not a Pinkerton," Starbuck said with a lame smile. "O'Brien was close, but I've never had anything to do with the Pinkertons. I work on my own."

"Your own?" she murmured uneasily. "Are you trying to tell me you're not a detective?"

"No," Starbuck confessed. "I'm a detective, but I run my own operation. I don't work for any of the big agencies."

"What's the difference?" Nell gave a dark, empty look. "You still conned me and fed me that line of hooey about Colorado."

"I'm not proud of it," Starbuck admitted. "I had a job to do and I went about it the best way I knew how. Maybe I conned you, but it wasn't like I had any real choice. It stuck in my craw the whole time."

"Go crap in your hat, buster! You wanted information, and you pumped me till the well ran dry. You got me hooked with your sweet talk and all the rest of that nonsense, and it never meant a thing to you. Nothing!"

"That's not true." Starbuck studied her downcast face. "The only lies I told you had to do with the job. Everything else was on the square." He lifted her chin, looked directly into her eyes. "The other part—what you're talking about—wasn't any lie. I meant every word of it."

"Honest to God?" She drew a deep, unsteady breath. "You're not just saying that? You really mean it?"

"Straight gospel," Starbuck said earnestly. "When I leave Frisco, you're going with me. You're through with O'Brien and the Barbary Coast and all the rest. That's a solid-gold promise."

Nell stared at him in an intense, haggard way. She was filled with conflicting emotions, and terrified that she might once again be played for a fool. Her lips trembled and she tried to smile, a tortured smile. There was a hungry, questing quality in her eyes, and she searched his face uncertainly. She wanted desperately to believe.

Then, suddenly, she stood within the circle of his arms. She shuddered convulsively against him and pressed her cheek to his chest. Her voice was muffled, almost a plea.

"I'm with you, lover. Where do we go from here?"

Starbuck took her shoulders and held her at arm's length. "You know I've got to get O'Brien and Adair, don't you?" She nodded dumbly, and he went on. "Then I want you to tell me where they've gone. Unless I'm wrong, time's running out fast."

"Once you've caught them, is it over? Will we be able to leave then, Harry?"

"You just pack your duds and wait for me. We're as good as on our way."

Nell briefly recounted everything she'd heard through the wall. Listening to her, Starbuck could generally reconstruct the sequence of events since Adair's escape at the farmhouse. It was no great surprise that everyone involved, Buckley included, now knew he was a detective. Yet one aspect of the situation left him troubled. Buckley's insistence that Adair depart San Francisco— or be killed—was ominous. The blind man quite obviously understood that the trail led to the Snug Café, and had taken measures to sever the link. Which meant there wasn't a moment to spare.

"That's all," Nell concluded. "Denny browbeat Ned into it, and I heard them leave a few minutes after it got dark."

"You mentioned Mother Bronson's joint. Who's she?"

"A witch who runs a dive on the waterfront. She shanghais sailors and sells them to captains of outbound ships. I guess Denny figured she would know which clippers are sailing tonight."

"Would O'Brien hang around until Adair ships out?"

"Probably," Nell said hesitantly. "From what I overheard, he wouldn't take any chances. Ned wasn't too keen on the idea."

"Then I reckon I'd better head for Mother Bronson's."

"Be careful," Nell cautioned. "She's tougher than most men on the Coast. And that includes Denny O'Brien."

"I'll watch myself."

Starbuck walked to the door and turned the key. With his hand on the knob, he stopped and looked around. "You be ready when I get back. Things are liable to happen fast when the fur starts to fly."

"I'll be waiting," she replied with a sudden sad grin. "I've no place to go without you, lover."

The door opened and closed, and he was gone.

A misty rain was falling, and the night was ripe with the smell of the sea. The streetlights were dim silvery globes, their lamps casting flickering shadows on the wet streets. Sailors, stumping along with the bowlegged gait peculiar to seamen, clogged the waterfront.

Starbuck walked toward Battery Point. Out in the

bay, anchored away from the wharves, were hundreds of ships. Their silhouettes were fuzzy through the mist and fog, but the ghostly assemblage indicated Frisco's importance as one of the world's major ports. The lanterns of small boats bobbed like fireflies on the rolling water. Known locally as Whitehall boats, the craft ferried sailors ashore for a fee. From there, once his foot touched dry land, the seaman ventured forth at his own peril.

Oceangoing ships, not to mention the men who sailed them, were a complete mystery to Starbuck. Yet the waterfront itself was infamous, with a reputation for danger and foul play known even to landlubbers. The Barbary Coast was rough and sordid, but altogether tame compared to the waterfront. Starbuck had few illusions about the hazards that lay ahead.

All along the wharves were a seedy collection of gaming dives, whorehouses, and busthead saloons. Vice was the stock in trade, and after months at sea, the sailors were victims of their own shipboard fantasies. On reaching port, Jack Tar set off in search of women, alcohol, and gambling. The wilder the women, the better, and even popskull whiskey was none too potent for a sailor with a thirst. Whether able seaman or galley cook, he had money and was eager to blow it on a nonstop, night-and-day spree. Waiting to accommodate him was an assortment of vultures in human form.

Those who operated the waterfront dives were specialists who dealt in live bodies. Their ostensible aim was to provide the seafearer with diverse forms of entertainment. Their principal business, however, was the traffic in shanghaied sailors. The seaman's origin, whether Scandinavian or German, French or British, was of no consequence. The first step was to fleece the sailor of his wages, either at the gaming tables or at the hands of bloozy whores. Then, once he was penniless, the bartender slipped him a drink drugged with sulphate of morphine. Afterward, the warm body was delivered to a ship captain who paid cash on the spot. The sailor awoke to find himself on a voyage that lasted two to four years. Though the practice was widespread, few seamen made any effort to avoid the waterfront. The danger of being shanghaied was considered one of the lesser hazards of shore leave in Frisco.

The Whale, a sleezy dive operated by Mother Bronson, was located at Battery Point. Crude even by Frisco standards, it was a saloon with girls for rent by the trick or by the hour. The ramshackle building squatted directly on the wharf, with water lapping at the pilings below. By rowboat, the trip from The Whale to a waiting clipper was only a matter of minutes. For the shanghaied seaman, it was also a one-way trip. The next port of call was generally halfway around the world.

Starbuck drew stares the moment he stepped through the door. The patrons of The Whale were rough-garbed sailors, rank with the smell of sweat and cheap whiskey. While few of them spoke the same language, they were all dressed similarly and appeared stamped from the same mold. By contrast, Starbuck looked like a peacock among a flock of guinea fowl. His powder-blue suit and pearl-gray fedora left a buzz of conversation in his wake.

Walking to the bar, he ordered whiskey and took his time lighting a cigar. He ignored the stares and the muttered comments, idly inspecting the room. Several house girls were working the crowd, but they held his interest only briefly. On the way to the waterfront, he had formulated a loose, though somewhat credible, cover story. With a glib line of patter, and a little name-dropping, he hoped to bluff his way past Mother Bronson. From there, depending on how the dice fell, he would attempt to take O'Brien and Adair without bloodshed. One elbow hooked over the bar, he sipped his drink and waited.

Presently, the door to a back room swung open. The woman who emerged was tall, with shoulders as wide as a man's, and had the stern look of a grenadier. Her hair was pulled back in a severe bun, and her drab dress somehow accentuated the massive bulk of her figure. A lead-loaded blackjack was wedged into the belt cinched around her waist. She looked entirely capable of felling man or beast with one blow.

Plowing through the crowd, she moved directly to the bar and stopped beside Starbuck. She sized him up, her beady eyes noting every detail of his gaudy attire. At last, with her hands on her hips, she rocked her head from side to side.

"Little out of your element, ain't you, sport?"

"You Mother Bronson?"

"That's the name." She gave a tight, mirthless smile. "Who's asking?"

"Johnny One-Spot." Starbuck thought the name had a certain ring. "I've got a message for Denny O'Brien."

"Oh, do you?" Her smirk widened into a smug grin. "And what makes you think you'd find him in a dump like this?"

"High Spade McQueen sent me." Starbuck knocked back his whiskey and wiped his mouth. "He said to tell you the plan's been changed. I'm to explain to O'Brien himself, and no one else."

"Are you, now?" She signaled the barkeep. "Have another drink, sport. We'll talk about it some and see where that takes us."

"What's to talk about?"

The barkeep brought another glass and the bottle.

His hand passed over Starbuck's glass, deftly opening and closing, as he poured for Mother Bronson. Then he filled Starbuck's glass and casually walked away.

"Well, Johnny One-Spot"—she lifted her glass—"here's mud in your eye."

She tossed down her drink and Starbuck followed suit. He puffed importantly on his cigar and looked impatient. "I haven't got all night. You gonna take me to Mr. O'Brien or not?"

There was the merest beat of hesitation. Then her smile broadened. "Tell you the truth, you haven't got hardly any time at all, sport."

"What the hell's that supposed to mean?"

"Ask me again when you wake up."

"When I—?"

Starbuck's eyes glazed and the cigar dropped from his mouth. He slumped against the bar, then staggered sideways, and his knees suddenly turned rubbery. He pitched face down on the floor.

Mother Bronson stooped, rolling him over, and took one of his legs under each arm. Effortlessly, she dragged him toward the rear of the saloon. One of her girls rushed to open the door and she disappeared into the back room. There, waiting silently, were Denny O'Brien and Ned Adair. She let go his legs and turned to O'Brien.

"Well, dearie, there's your man. Colder'n a mackerel!"

"No," O'Brien said, staring down a moment. "I think he's Ned's man. Call it a going-away present."

"Present!" Adair repeated with a quizzical look. "You want me to take him with me?"

"Only partway." OBrien smiled evilly. "Feed him to the sharks once you get out to sea."

Mother Bronson threw back her head and roared with laughter.

Starbuck awoke to a curious yawing motion. His vision was blurred and his head felt as though it had been cleaved down the middle. Several moments elapsed before his eyes cleared and he was able to collect himself. Sitting up, he gazed around and slowly realized he was in a cargo hold. Then, with sudden clarity, it struck him.

He was on a ship! A clipper ship bound for the Orient!

His last recollection was of Mother Bronson. Everything afterward was a blank, but not too difficult to piece together. He'd walked into a trap, with Denny O'Brien very likely watching from the back room. Then, like a prize sucker, he'd never given it a second thought when Mother Bronson called for another round of drinks. Yet he hadn't been shanghaied. Nothing so simple would satisfy O'Brien. The orders, without doubt, were to kill him and dump his body at sea.

He cursed himself for a fool. Standing, his hand went to the shoulder holster and found it empty. He lifted his pants leg and discovered they'd missed the hideout gun in his boot top. The stubby Colt was a last-ditch weapon, but deadly at short ranges. The thought occurred that it was his one hope for deliverance, and he reminded himself to make every shot count. He cocked the hammer and moved toward a ladder at the rear of the hold.

On deck, he saw that he was amidships. The rain had stopped, and stars were visible through occasional gaps in the clouds. Off the port side, far in the distance, he spotted a flashing light and the broken outline of a land mass. He realized with a start that the clipper was approaching the Golden Gate. Only minutes separated the ship from the open sea.

Crouching down, he scuttled toward the railing on the port side. Then, growing closer, he heard voices from the quarterdeck. The shadowed figures of two men appeared out of the dark. One, wearing a billed cap, was clearly a ship's officer. The other, who paused at the stairway, was Red Ned Adair. Starbuck froze, watching them intently.

"You're the captain," Adair remarked testily. "But the sooner we toss him overboard, the better I'll like it."

"I've no quarrel with that, Mr. Adair. As I told you, after we've cleared land's end, you can do as you please."

Adair grunted and started down the stairway leading to the main deck. Then, squinting hard, he suddenly saw Starbuck crouched low in the dark. His jaw popped open in a startled cry.

"Lovett—!"

The captain and Ned Adair went for their guns in the same motion. Starbuck leveled his arm and the snubby Colt spat three times. The slugs stitched an oval pattern in Adair's chest, and he tumbled down the stairway. A bullet tugged at the sleeve of Starbuck's jacket, and he saw the captain staring at him over the sights of a bulldog revolver. His arm moved and the Colt recoiled twice in quick succession. One slug punched into the captain's stomach, the other ripped through his throat and tore out the back of his skull. The impact flung him backward and he dropped raglike on the quarterdeck.

The helmsman shouted, and the thud of footsteps from below decks galvanized Starbuck to action. Working frantically, he stuffed the Colt in the waistband of his trousers and jerked off his boots. Then, in two swift strides, he crossed the deck and dove headlong over the railing. The shock of the icy water struck him like a blow, and a moment later he knifed cleanly to the surface. Bobbing about in the waves, he somehow got his bearings, and saw the flash of a beacon far astern.

A wayward thought seized him, and he vaguely wondered if sharks attacked in the dark. Then, with a stoic sense of fatalism, he dismissed it from mind. He turned into the tide and swam toward the distant light.

Chapter Sixteen

The sky was like tarnished pewter, heavy with clouds. False dawn left the alleyway obscured in gloom, and a murky stillness hung over the street. Starbuck checked behind him, then rounded the corner of the Bella Union and halted at the kitchen door. He took out a pocket-knife and began working on the lock.

His nerves were gritty and raw, and his head pounded with a dull, grinding weariness. The long swim, some four miles through bone-chilling seas, had sapped his strength to the very marrow. He'd come ashore at Point Lobos, and from there made his way to the Cliff House, a fashionable restaurant on the oceanfront. The manager, shaken by the sight of a waterlogged apparition, had loaned him a driver and carriage, and sent him off wrapped in a woolly blanket. Warm at last, he'd stretched out on the seat and slept during the ride back to the city. When the driver let him off at the hotel, he had felt somewhat restored, though still a bit unsteady on his feet. A hot bath and a change of clothes had improved his spirits, if not the lingering sense of exhaustion. Then, on the point of leaving the room, he'd suddenly remembered an old friend, packed away in his suitcase. He walked out of the hotel with the Colt .45 jammed in a crossdraw holster.

Now, probing at the lock, his one concern was Nell. He could only surmise that she was still in her room, waiting for him to return. She was levelheaded, no stranger to tight situations, and he thought it unlikely she would have betrayed herself to O'Brien. It was reasonable to assume she had worked her normal shift, and resisted the temptation to ask questions. Yet, given the circumstances, the night would have proved an ordeal. Her position was untenable, hinging on a slip of the tongue, and by now the pressure would have taken its toll. She wouldn't be safe until he had her clear of the Bella Union, and out of harm's way. Only then would he turn his attention to Denny O'Brien.

The tumbler in the lock abruptly clicked and he eased through the door. He moved across the empty kitchen, with scarcely a glance at the dumbwaiter. He was cautious, but not overly concerned. With sunrise still an hour away, not even the swampers would have begun work. He followed a passageway toward the front of the building, and emerged through a door near the end of the bar. There he stopped, senses alert, listening.

The barroom was still as a graveyard. He waited several moments, one ear cocked to any noise, then walked to the staircase. On the second floor he paused again, but saw no one and heard nothing. Another flight up, he flattened against the wall and edged one step at a time onto the third-floor landing. After a while, he proceeded gingerly along the hall. He ghosted past McQueen's room, and then, opposite the door to O'Brien's suite, he suddenly went stock-still. From inside, he heard the low drone of voices. Insofar as he could determine, there were only two men, quite probably O'Brien and McQueen. He briefly considered busting through the door and taking them prisoner. On second thought, however, he rejected the idea. Any commotion would arouse others, and make it impossible for him to spirit Nell out of the Bella Union. Her safety, for the moment, took priority over all else. Besides, O'Brien believed he was dead, snugly tucked away in some shark's belly. Time enough to disabuse him of that notion later in the day. All the time in the world, once Nell was out of danger.

On tiptoe, alert to creaky floorboards, he made his way to the end of the hall. He paused in front of Nell's room, debating whether to rap softly, then decided to try the doorknob. It turned, and he swiftly ducked inside, closing the door behind him. The latch clicked and in the same instant his guts turned to stone.

Nell lay sprawled on the floor. Her arms were akimbo, her hair loose and fanned darkly across her face. The bodice of her dress was torn, exposing her breasts, and her skirt was hitched up over her legs. She seemed too still, deathly still.

Starbuck scooped her up in his arms and carried her to the bed. Only then, with streamers of light flooding through the window, was her condition aparent. She had been beaten, expertly and brutally, with methodical savagery. Her nose was broken, her lips puffy and discolored, and her left eye was swollen shut. As he lowered her onto the bed, she groaned and her good eye slowly rolled open. Her mouth ticced upward in a ghastly smile.

"Harry."

"Don't try to talk."

"You came back for me."

"Told you I would." Starbuck forced himself to

177

smile, leaning closer. "Now, you rest easy and let me have a look at you."

He gently brushed the hair out of her face. Unwitingly, moved by some urge to touch her, he placed his hand on her waist. She recoiled, and a sharp spasm of pain distorted her features. Her mouth opened in a wheezing moan and frothy red bubbles leaked down over her chin. She gasped, laboring desperately to get her breath.

Starbuck knew then her condition was beyond hope. Her rib cage was shattered, and the bloody froth told the tale. One lung, perhaps both, had been punctured. From the punishment she'd absorbed, blows that hard, it seemed entirely likely her insides were torn apart. A veteran of death and dying, he recognized all the signs. The life force was quickly draining out of her, and she hadn't one chance in a thousand. Which was one step removed from zero.

"Nell," Starbuck said softly. "Can you hear me?"

Her eye fluttered open. The agonized look subsided, and she struggled to bring him into focus. Her head moved in a slight nod.

"Was it O'Brien? Did he do this to you?"

"No." Her voice was weak. "He sicced McQueen on me."

"Why?"

"He knew I was"—she grimaced, caught her breath—"only one who could've told you . . . Mother Bronson's."

"He let McQueen work you over because of that?"

"Doesn't matter." She blinked, her eye suddenly brighter. "I waited, and you're here now."

"I'm sorry," Starbuck said hollowly. "I got back as fast as I could."

"Harry, do something for me?"

178

"Anything," Starbuck told her. "You name it, and it's yours."

"Don't leave me here."

"I won't."

"Take me with you—to Colorado—the way we . . ."

Her voice trailed off and her mouth parted in a shuddering sigh. Then her eye rolled back in her head, and she stopped breathing. She died within the space of a heartbeat.

Starbuck tenderly closed her eye and sat for a long while holding her hand. Finally, prying her fingers loose, he stood and squared himself up. He realized he'd wanted to tell her his real name, and felt some loss that there had been no time. A slow sense of rage, fueled by his own shame, settled over him. His mouth hardened, and the rage turned to quiet steel fury. He pulled the Colt and walked quickly to the door. Without looking back, he stepped into the hall.

The murmur of voices was still audible from O'Brien's suite. Starbuck quietly tested the doorknob, then braced himself and swung the door wide. He barged into the sitting room, the Colt extended and cocked, and kicked the door shut. O'Brien was seated in an armchair, and McQueen was lounged back on a nearby sofa. A bottle, almost three-quarters empty, and a couple of glasses stood on a table between them. O'Brien's face went chalky.

"Lovett!"

"Just call me Lazarus." Starbuck's eyes were cold, impassive. "Only your boys never quite put me down for the count."

"What—" O'Brien faltered, staring at him with open disbelief. "How'd you get away from Adair?"

"Simple," Starbuck said lazily. "I killed him."

McQueen slowly rose to his feet. His jacket was

splattered with flecks of blood, and the knuckles on his right hand were skinned raw. Starbuck wagged the barrel of the Colt in his direction.

"Don't get sudden."

"What the hell; you got the drop on me."

"All the same," Starbuck said shortly, "any funny moves and you'd better take a deep breath. It'll have to last a long time."

"You talk big with a gun in your hand."

"Give me an excuse and I'll fix it so you won't have to listen anymore."

"Hold off, Mac!" O'Brien interjected quickly. "He's got nothing on us."

"Think not?" Starbuck eyed him keenly. "Let's just say I've got all I need and then some."

O'Brien laughed. "With Adair dead, your case is out the window. There's no way you can tie me to those train holdups."

"I had something better in mind."

"Yeah, like what?"

Starbuck's gaze bored into him. "For openers, we'll take a walk down to your office. Then you're going to show me the ledgers you've got locked in your safe."

"Ledgers?" O'Brien went white around the mouth. "You're off your rocker! Those are my books for the Bella Union. The house accounts."

"No," Starbuck said with wry contempt. "I'd lay odds one of them is your insurance policy against Buckley. You're too slick not to keep a record of the payoffs."

"In a pig's ass!" O'Brien fixed him with a baleful look. "Even if there were payoffs, why would I keep a record?"

"A little something in reserve, something to hold over Buckley's head. The way he operates, you know you'd need it sooner or later. I figure you've got enough to convict him a dozen times over."

O'Brien peered at him, one eye sharp and gleaming. "What's your game, Lovett? Pinkertons don't get involved with political shenanigans. Maybe you're looking for a payoff yourself."

A ferocious grin suddenly lit Starbuck's face. "You'd be surprised about us Pinkertons. There's a payoff, all right, but it's not exactly what you had in mind."

"What d' you mean?"

"A rough guess would be twenty years. You and Buckley ought to make perfect cellmates. Two peas in a pod."

"Guess again!" O'Brien eyes glazed with rage. "You've got bats in the belfry if you think I'm gonna hand over those ledgers. I'll see you in hell first!"

"Don't take it so hard," Starbuck taunted. "There's lots of things worse than twenty years."

"How about me?" McQueen gave him a humorless yellow-toothed smile. "You gonna send me to the rockpile, too?"

"Nope." Starbuck's faded blue eyes narrowed. "You're something special, McQueen. You've got a date with the hangman."

"Hangman!" A sourly amused look came over Mc-Queen's face. "Who the hell am I supposed to've murdered?"

"Nell," Starbuck said quietly. "She died a couple of minutes ago."

McQueen scowled with stuffed-animal ferocity. He read the expression in Starbuck's eyes, and saw revealed there a cold, implacable truth. He would never live to reach the police station, much less a trial by jury. He had already been judged and sentenced. And before him stood a self-appointed executioner.

O'Brien suddenly rose from his chair. The movement momentarily distracted Starbuck, and McQueen took the only chance open to him. With an unintelligible oath, his hand snaked inside his coat and reappeared with a Sharps derringer. An instant before he could bring the gun to bear, Starbuck fired. The first round, a hurried snap-shot, caught him in the shoulder. Knocked off balance, he slammed backward and sat down heavily on the sofa. The second slug drilled through his sternum and the third struck him squarely in the heart. He sat bolt upright a moment, then the light flickered and died in his eyes. The derringer slipped from his grasp and he slumped dead on the sofa.

Starbuck crossed the room in two swift strides. He patted O'Brien down, relieving him of a belly gun, and tossed it on the chair. Then, in a quick, savage gesture, he motioned with the Colt.

"Let's get that safe open. Any tricks—anyone tries to stop us—and you'll wind up on the meatwagon. Savvy?"

O'Brien nodded sullenly. "No tricks."

"You lead the way."

Several minutes later they emerged from the Bella Union. O'Brien had the ledgers under his arm and the snout of a Colt pressed against his spine. Starbuck flagged a hansom cab and shoved him inside. After a word with the driver, Starbuck stepped into the cab and seated himself. He kept the pistol trained on O'Brien's stomach.

"What now?" O'Brien asked as the cab pulled away from the curb. "Where're you taking me?"

Starbuck's expression was sphinxlike. "You'll see when we get there."

"What's the harm in telling me? It's the police station, isn't it? You're gonna have them lock me up."

"You'd like that, wouldn't you? By suppertime, Buckley would have you sprung and on the next clipper to China."

O'Brien's jaw muscles worked. "What d'you want, Lovett? You've got the goddamned ledgers. Isn't that enough?"

"Not near enough," Starbuck said levelly. "We're headed for a warehouse, down at the train yard. We'll have it all to ourselves, just you and me. One way or another, I figure today's your day to turn songbird."

"Songbird?" A vein in O'Brien's temple stood out like twisted cord. "You want me to rat on Buckley?"

"That's the idea," Starbuck said, motioning with the Colt. "Those ledgers are only part of the story. Your testimony ought to cap it off real nice."

"It'll never happen! Denny O'Brien don't rat on nobody!"

"Wanna bet?" Starbuck regarded him evenly. "You'll talk . . . or else."

"Or else what?" O'Brien demanded. "You're not fooling anyone, Lovett. I'm no good to you dead, and we both know it."

"It's the other way round." Starbuck gave him a strange, crooked smile. "Unless you talk, you're no good to me alive. Think of it a while, and you'll see what I mean."

O'Brien saw a catlike eagerness in his eyes. Suddenly, as though his ears had come unplugged, the Barbary Coast boss got the message. Harry Lovett wanted to kill him, and would, given the slightest pretext. Which mean that his life, from that moment forward, had only one measure of value. So long as he testified, he would be allowed to go on breathing. His decision, considering the alternative, was really quite simple.

He decided to sing like a golden-throated canary.

Early that evening Starbuck walked from the train terminal and hailed a cab. Thus far, all the pieces had fallen into place, and he thought it might be wiser to quit while he was ahead. Yet one step remained, and he was determined to try. He ordered the driver to take him to Chinatown.

His day had been hectic, but rewarding. Denny O'Brien, under questioning, had proved himself a veritable gold mine of information. Once he began talking, it became apparent he had something bordering on total recall. He revealed names and dates and places, and, in most instances, tied them to events that established an unassailable time frame. Those slight lapses of memory he suffered were easily brought to light by the ledgers. There, too, the evidence was overwhelming. With meticulous care, he had entered every payoff, noting the date and the amount, along with the percentage of gross take from various Barbary Coast operations. The entries, itemized in O'Brien's laborious scrawl, covered prostitution and gambling as well as the all-pervasive protection racket. The ledgers substantiated that Christopher Buckley had shared in the proceeds to the tune of more than $1,000,000.

Late that afternoon, after taking a deposition from O'Brien, Starbuck had at last notified Charles Crocker. Shortly thereafter, a squad of Central Pacific security guards reported to the warehouse. O'Brien was sequestered in a windowless room, and men were posted both inside and outside the building. Their orders were direct and without equivocation. Anyone who attempted forcible entry to the warehouse was to be shot on the spot.

When Starbuck departed the warehouse, he'd had no qualms about O'Brien's safety. Nor any concern that his songbird would try to fly away.

On the Street of a Thousand Lanterns, a crowd was gathered outside Fung Jing Toy's house. A policeman was posted at the door, and a paddy wagon stood at curbside. Starbuck paid the hansom driver, then eased through the throng of Chinese who stared silently, almost expectantly, at the front door. He approached the policeman and nodded amiably.

"What's all the commotion?"

"Oh, would you believe it?" the officer replied in a thick brogue. "The big Chink himself has done been murdered."

"Fung Jing Toy?"

"Aye, the very one," the officer observed solemnly. "God rest his heathen soul."

The door opened, and a murmur swept through the crowd. Several policemen, formed in a protective wedge, escorted two Chinese down the steps and hustled them into the paddy wagon. Starbuck instantly recognized the men, Wong Yee and Sing Dock. The last time he'd seen them they were guarding the entrance to Fung's underground chamber.

"Are those the killers?"

"Caught red-handed," the officer affirmed. "And them the Chink's own *boo how doy*. Cut him to ribbons with their hatchets, they did. Terrible sight. Terrible."

Starbuck turned and walked away. Somehow he wasn't surprised by Fung Jing Toy's death. Some dark complex of gut instinct and premonition had warned him that Buckley would move swiftly. With Denny O'Brien in custody, Mr. Frisco couldn't risk the possibility of still another turncoat. All the more imperative, Fung represented a corroborative witness, the one man who could substantiate O'Brien's testimony. Buckley, expedient to the end, had simply ordered the Chinaman's assassination.

Yet Starbuck was surprised by the choice of assassins. Wong Yee and Sing Dock were clearly the tools of Christopher Buckley. Their loyalty to a white-devil overlord, rather than Fung, confirmed Buckley's absolute domination of the Chinatown tongs. Still, while a key witness had been silenced, the blind man had no reason for celebration. He was, ironically enough, very much in the dark.

The ledgers were the one element Buckley couldn't have foreseen, and never suspected. A mute form of corroboration that spoke louder than words.

Mr. Frisco was shortly due the shock of his life.

Chapter Seventeen

"Perhaps you could elaborate, Mr. Starbuck."

"Well, in a manner of speaking, you might liken it to the links in a chain. Adair led me to O'Brien, who in turn led me to Fung. From there, things led straight to Buckley. He was the last link in the chain."

"You refer to Christopher A. Buckley, proprietor of the Snug Café. Is that correct?"

"Correct."

"Now, you used the analogy—links in a chain. Would you consider it valid to broaden the analogy, and call it a chain of command?"

"Yes, I would," Starbuck agreed. "It was organized along military lines. Fung and O'Brien were like field commanders, with their own sector of operations. They were free to run things to suit themselves, but they were responsible for their actions. In other words, they reported to a higher authority."

"So Fung controlled Chinatown and O'Brien controlled the Barbary Coast. They operated independently on day-to-day matters, but they were answerable for the overall results in their sectors. Is that essentially correct?"

"Yes."

"Would you consider it a fair statement to characterize Christopher Buckley as their commander-in-chief?"

"I would," Starbuck acknowledged. "He appointed them, and he could strip them of command any time he took a notion. His orders were the last word."

"By that, you mean there was no appeal?"

"None whatever. He was the last link in the chain, and his word was final. It all stopped there."

The Grand Jury room, located in the Hall of Justice, went silent. The jurors were attentive, listening raptly, their eyes fixed on Starbuck. They gazed at him with the look of circus spectators watching a tiger eat its keeper. From the news stories, they knew he had killed three men during the course of his assignment in San Francisco. Hushed and eager, they waited to hear more.

Edgar Caldwell, the district attorney, paused for dramatic effect. He adjusted his spectacles, and stood for a moment consulting his notes. An ambitious man, he was commonly thought to be a force in county politics. Yet his conduct of the hearing indicated he was putting distance between himself and Buckley's local machine. He was seeking an indictment, but on the man rather than the Democratic Party. At length, he turned back to the witness chair.

"Mr. Starbuck, a minute ago you testified that—and I quote—things led straight to Buckley. What did you mean by 'things'?"

Starbuck wormed around in his chair. With a straight face, he briefly recounted his cover story, and the offer to buy one hundred Chinese slave girls. Then he told of Fung's suspicions, which led ultimately to the meeting with Buckley. He concluded with a short synopsis of the meeting, and Buckley's open admission of power.

"Let's be clear on that point," Caldwell insisted. "Buckley stated that he'd been asked to arbitrate the matter?"

"Yes."

"Then he went on to state that he would approve the deal—the sale of a hundred Chinese virgins—if your references were in order. Isn't that correct?"

"So far as it goes," Starbuck amended. "I also had to show good faith by putting up a hundred thousand in cash."

"Which you obtained from your employer, Charles Crocker?"

"That's right."

"To recap, Mr. Starbuck." Caldwell struck an elegant pose for the jurors. "Buckley dictated the terms necessary to consummate the deal, and he then imposed those terms on both Fung and O'Brien. Is that your testimony?"

"Yes, it is."

"Have you any direct knowledge of why Fung and O'Brien would comply with his demands?"

"I do," Starbuck nodded. "O'Brien called him Mr. Frisco. He stated that Buckley could approve or disapprove the deal, and everybody would just have to live with the decision. The question at issue—and Buckley confirmed this in our meeting—was how to conclude the deal and still keep peace between Fung and O'Brien."

"If I may paraphrase," Caldwell said, one eye on the jurors. "Buckley would hand down his edict, and his henchmen, Fung and O'Brien, would have no choice but to obey. A fair summation of the facts?"

"In a nutshell, that's the way it worked."

"Very well, Mr. Starbuck. Suppose we move on. In previous testimony, one Dennis O'Brien identified a certain set of ledgers. He stated that one ledger in particular dealt with payoffs to Buckley, as regards criminal activities on the Barbary Coast. Are you familiar with the ledgers in question?"

"I personally observed O'Brien take those ledgers from his office safe in the Bella Union."

"So the ledgers were intact—all entries previously recorded—at that time?"

"Yes."

"Did O'Brien voluntarily surrender the ledgers?"

"No." Starbuck smiled. "I forced him to open the safe at gunpoint."

"Please describe the events that transpired immediately thereafter."

"I took O'Brien to a warehouse . . ."

Starbuck's testimony consumed the better part of an hour. When he was finished, Caldwell excused him from the witness chair and thanked him profusely. The jurors sat spellbound as he walked from the room. Their expressions indicated they believed the man, and the story he'd told.

Outside, moving along the corridor, he felt an enormous sense of relief. Three weeks had elapsed since the capture of Denny O'Brien and the death of Fung Jing Toy. In that time, waiting for a grand jury to be empaneled, he had worked closely with the district attorney. His continued presence had also worked as an influence on O'Brien. The Barbary Coast boss had cooperated fully, and turned state's evidence in exchange for a reduced sentence. A convincing witness, he had testified earlier in the day. And along with his ledgers, he'd apparently made an impression on the jurors.

There now seemed little doubt as to the outcome. An indictment would be forthcoming, and Buckley would stand trial on charges ranging from criminal conspiracy to accessory to murder. Conviction would very likely put him behind bars for the rest of his life.

For Starbuck, it was the end to a long and trying period. He had enjoyed the chase, and felt great personal accomplishment at having brought Mr. Frisco to bay. Still, there were bad memories as well, and a change of scenery seemed very much in order. His thoughts turned to Denver.

Then, rounding the corner into the lobby, he abruptly stopped. Christopher Buckley, being led by another man, appeared through the front entrance and walked toward him. He recalled Buckley was scheduled to testify before the grand jury, and briefly considered not speaking. But upon second thought, he changed his mind. A last word with the blind man seemed a fitting end to the case.

"Afternoon, Mr. Buckley."

"Good afternoon." Buckley halted, his expression quizzical. "I'm afraid you have the advantage of me."

"Luke Starbuck," Starbuck replied with a ghost of a grin. "Otherwise known as Harry Lovett."

"Of course!" Buckley said, smiling faintly. "How could I ever forget that voice?"

"Yeah, I reckon a voice is pretty hard to disguise."

"Well, that's past us now, Mr. Starbuck. I understand you've even dispensed with your gold tooth."

"Oh?" Starbuck asked pleasantly. "Keeping tabs on me, are you?"

Buckley's smile turned cryptic. "You remember

my associate, Knuckles Jackson? He keeps me up to date on the latest newspaper accounts of your activities. All the more so since you've become such a celebrity."

Starbuck and Jackson traded nods. A large man, Jackson had a square and pugnacious face, with cold gun-metal eyes. For a moment, Starbuck couldn't place him. Then, suddenly, he recalled the night O'Brien and McQueen had escorted him to the Snug Café. Jackson was the resident gorilla who guarded the alley door. His presence here today spoke for itself. He was apparently trusted to act as Buckley's seeing-eye dog and chief bodyguard.

"Funny thing," Starbuck said, glancing back at Buckley. "All this hoopla about me doesn't amount to a hill of beans. I've got an idea you're the one they'll remember."

"On the contrary!" Buckley's tone was lordly, somehow patronizing. "You shouldn't be so modest, Mr. Starbuck. The public loves to be titillated, and you've certainly shown them the seamier side of San Francisco. Small wonder it's captured their imagination."

"Here today, gone tomorrow," Starbuck said lightly. "People forget real quick."

"True," Buckley said with an indulgent smile. "Fame rides a fleet horse. Nonetheless, you're to be congratulated on a splendid job. You have a few peers in your particular line of work."

Starbuck tried to divine his mood. For a man facing prison, he was altogether too congenial, and far too unconcerned. His excessively reasonable tone somehow rang false. Then, too, there was something strange about his expression. Behind the tinted glasses, the dead eyes seemed oddly mocking, alight with laughter. The effect was unsettling, vaguely unnatural.

"I admire the way you're taking it all in stride, Mr. Buckley."

"Why not?" Buckley spread his hands in a bland gesture. "Life is very much like a melodrama, Mr. Starbuck. Look closely and you'll find that pathos and farce always merge in the end. What appears to be reality is often little more than illusion."

"I wouldn't know about that," Starbuck remarked. "Course, just from the sound of it, I get the feeling you're not losing any sleep over this grand jury business."

"You tell me," Buckley said almost idly. "Should I be losing sleep?"

"You're on your way to testify, aren't you?"

"Indeed I am."

"Then I reckon you'll be able to answer the question yourself. There's no illusion so far as the jurors are concerned. It's all hard fact."

"So I hear," Buckley said, not without bitterness. "O'Brien and his ledgers apparently make for a convincing tale."

Starbuck regarded his somberly. "You must have inside sources. Those ledgers were a pretty well-kept secret."

"People talk," Buckley replied absently. "A secret ceases to be a secret once it's known by a second party. But, of course, that's hardly news to a man in your profession."

"No, I guess not." Starbuck nodded, acknowledging the truth of the statement. "Leastways, I never had any trouble getting people to talk about you."

Buckley smiled humorlessly. "Come now, Mr. Starbuck. Denny O'Brien talked because you put a gun to his head. Except for that, you would never have gotten past the stage of speculation and conjecture."

"Maybe so," Starbuck admitted. "The way it worked out, we'll never know. He talked, and that's all that counts."

"Ah, yes," Buckley commented loftily. "The hard facts you spoke of a moment ago."

"Hard facts," Starbuck said slowly, emphatically, "and all down in black and white."

"You believe they'll indict me, then?"

"Let's just say I'd lay odds on it."

"A sporting man to the end, hmm?"

"No, I only bet on sure things."

"Touché," Buckley said equably. "And what of you, Mr. Starbuck. Where to now that your terrible swift sword has done its work?"

"Another town, another job," Starbuck countered easily. "There's so many crooks around, it keeps a fellow in my line pretty much on the go."

"Indeed?" Buckley paused as though weighing his words. "Another town, another job sounds imminently practical, Mr. Starbuck. Allow me to wish you good hunting . . . elsewhere."

"Some men might take that as a threat."

"Perhaps." Buckley smiled without warmth. "I'm sure you'll take it in the spirit in which it was intended, Mr. Starbuck."

Starbuck laughed and gave him an offhand salute. With a nod to Knuckles Jackson, he walked to the front entrance and pushed through the door. Outside, he found the way barred by a gang of reporters and several newspaper cameramen. For all the publicity surrounding the case, he had thus far avoided both interviews and photographs. Today, with the grand jury in session, the press cast aside any pretense of civility. Camera powder flashed and reporters swarmed forward, peppering him with questions.

"What's the latest, Mr. Starbuck?"

"No comment."

"Will they indict Buckley?"

"Your guess is as good as mine."

"C'mon, be a sport. Give us the lowdown!"

"I only know what I read in the papers."

"Can we quote you on that?"

"Suit yourself."

"Have a heart, Mr. Starbuck! We're only trying to do our job!"

"No comment."

To a chorus of groans and invidious remarks, Starbuck brushed past them. He hurried down the steps and walked toward Kearny Street. A moment later he disappeared around the corner.

Early the next morning Starbuck was ushered into Charles Crocker's office. The railroad tycoon greeted him wth an ebullient smile and a bear-trap handshake. Once they were seated, Crocker tossed a newspaper across the desk.

"Have you seen that?"

"Yeah, I read it at breakfast."

Starbuck's photo stared back at him from the front page. Emblazoned across the top was a bold headline, which in itself told the story. The grand jury had indicted Christopher Buckley on all counts.

"You did it!" Crocker boomed out jovially. "By Christ, you said you would—and you did!"

"I got lucky."

"Luck, hell!" Crocker beamed. "Nobody gets his picture on every front page in town because he's lucky. You pulled off a feat of detection that's unrivaled. You're the toast of San Francisco!"

"So I read."

The irony of the moment wasn't lost on Starbuck. Crocker, not quite a month ago, had strenuously opposed the plan to expose Buckley. Yet now, basking in the reflected glory, he was something of a hero himself. His statements to the newspapers implied that the Central Pacific Railroad was in large measure responsible for Buckley's downfall. The idea struck Starbuck as amusing. All the more so since Crocker was now portraying himself as a paragon of civic virtue. He thought it a strange and unlikely role for a robber baron.

"Yessir," Crocker said with vinegary satisfaction, "you nailed Chris Buckley to the cross, and we all owe you a vote of thanks. San Francisco won't ever be the same again!"

Starbuck shrugged off the compliment. "I just did my job."

"Your job and then some!" Crocker said, jubilant. "You called Buckley and his crowd spoilers, and you were right. I'll have to admit I wasn't sold on the idea, not at first. But you turned me around, Luke. You made me see the light!" His voice rose triumphantly. "This is a proud day for the Central Pacific. A proud day!"

"Speaking of trains," Starbuck said wryly, "I've got to get a move on. I aim to catch the eastbound out of Oakland this evening."

"Eastbound?" Crocker suddenly looked perplexed. "Where are you going?"

"Denver," Starbuck said with a tired smile. "That's my headquarters, and I've got business to look after."

Crocker pursed his lips, solemn. "The Central Pacific needs a new chief of security. Any chance you would consider it assuming I made it worth your while, stock options and that sort of thing?"

"Thanks all the same." Starbuck shook his head. "I appreciate the offer, but I'm not what you'd call a team man. I work best alone."

"I suspected as much," Crocker said with exaggerated gravity. "You will return for Buckley's trial, won't you? I understand it's been set for the spring court docket."

"Wouldn't miss it for the world."

"I should hope not!" Crocker frowned uncertainly. "O'Brien alone will never convict him. Your testimony is vital."

"I'll be here," Starbuck assured him. "You've got my word on it."

Crocker took a bank draft from inside a folder on his desk. "I intended to give you this, anyway. A bonus, so to speak." He leaned forward, extending the draft. "Perhaps it will also ensure your return for the trial."

Starbuck accepted the draft, studying it a moment. Then he looked up with some surprise. "Ten thousand is mighty generous. I would've settled for what you owed me and no bones either way."

"You earned it." Crocker laughed a short, mirthless laugh. "Ten dead men at a thousand dollars a head seems to me a rare bargain."

"Eleven." Starbuck gave him a lopsided grin. "Course, the farmer didn't rightly count. He just got in the way of a stray bullet."

"Nonetheless, he was a member of the gang. It appears I owe you another thousand, Luke."

"I'll collect when I see you in the spring."

"Done!" Crocker trumpeted. "Here's my hand on it!"

Starbuck rose and shook hands. Then, after a parting

word, he walked from the office. On his way to the elevator, he stuck the bank draft in his wallet and chuckled softly to himself. A thousand dollars a head was no bargain. He'd killed men for lots less, simply because they needed killing.

And in the end, someone had to kill them.

Chapter Eighteen

There was a slight chill in the air and fog obscured the waterfront. Farther away, beyond the city, a wintry sunset slowly settled into the ocean.

Starbuck stood on the fantail of the ferry. His eyes were fixed upon distance, faraway and clouded. A roll-your-own was stuck in the corner of his mouth, and he smoked without haste. San Francisco, quickly falling astern, was lost within some deeper reflection. His thoughts were on men, and events.

On the whole, he felt he'd done a creditable job. The band of train robbers and their leader had been exterminated. Fung Jing Toy dead, leaving Chinatown in turmoil. O'Brien, who most assuredly deserved killing, would nonetheless emerge from prison an old and withered shadow of the man who had once ruled the Barbary Coast. Christopher Buckley would be convicted and die an inmate, blind and ultimately enfeebled, in some dank prison cell. So what began as a routine assignment had ended with the downfall of Frisco's underworld hierarchy. A certain pride in a job well done was by no means out of order.

Yet, with some cynicism, Starbuck saw the darker side as well. In his view, there was no logical progression in human affairs. There were merely tides of change borne on violence and an endless upheaval of political structures. The winners hung the losers—or carted them off to prison—and things went on much as they always had and always would. The evils of man, corruption and greed, were the single constant. And in one of the stranger quirks of life, a man bursting with virtue was often less esteemed than the spoilers. The voters, for all their sanctimonious tommyrot, understood greed and willfully sought those pleasures that were considered wicked and depraved. A reformer, therefore, lasted only a short while. The spoilers went on forever.

Viewed from that perspective, the only change wrought would be a change in names and faces. A new political kingpin would step into the void and quickly replace Buckley. Another thug would batter his fellow thugs into submission, and emerge the czar of the Barbary Coast. The tong wars of Chinatown would produce yet another vice lord, and the market in Oriental slave girls would continue to flourish. A whole new cast of characters would rise to ascendancy in Frisco's underworld. And soon, from the waterfront to the Uptown Tenderloin, it would return to business as usual.

Still, all things considered, those were problems San Francisco would have to solve for itself. Starbuck saw his own role clearly, and moral judgments, while an engaging exercise, were not his bailiwick. He was a detective, not a civic crusader. He'd been hired to rout a gang of train robbers, and Red Ned Adair was dead.

Case closed.

From one standpoint, however, the case would never be closed. Over breakfast that morning, while reading the *Examiner,* he'd realized how fully the Frisco job had altered his own future. His testimony before the grand jury, and the attendant publicity, had resulted in his photo being splashed across the front pages of newspapers throughout the West. His anonymity, always an edge in past cases, was gone forever. Once a face in the crowd, he would now be known and recognized wherever he traveled. Coupled with his reputation, that loss of anonymity might shorten his life span considerably.

The upshot seemed equally clear to Starbuck. Now, more than ever, he must become a master of disguise. A man of a thousand faces, none of them his own. An undercover operative in every sense of the word. In short, a detective and a chameleon, all rolled into one.

Unbidden, the memory of Nell popped into his head. Since the night of her death, she had never been far from his thoughts. Not that he wanted to remember, or made any conscious effort to do so. Quite the contrary, the hurt and the shame were emotions yet to be reconciled. Whenever possible, he nudged all thought of her to some dark corner of his mind. Yet, despite his attempts to forget, she was always there. A vision too easily summoned, and a reminder of things lost forever.

With the clarity of hindsight, he understood he'd overplayed his hand. That night, when he'd left her alone at the Bella Union, he was supremely confident. No doubt existed that he would shortly capture Ned Adair and return to spirit her away from the Barbary Coast. He was cocky, altogether too sure of himself, and in his blind rush to get the job done, he had sadly underestimated Denny O'Brien. In effect, he had gambled Nell's life on the assumption he could outsmart a pack of cutthroats and thieves who were already wise to his game. And he'd lost.

That was the part he couldn't forget. To risk his own life was one thing. He was, after all, being paid to accept whatever risk the job entailed. To risk Nell's life was another matter entirely. Her only stake in the game was a fabrication of lies and promises. In the end, of course, he would never have welched completely on their arrangement. He fully intended to take her away from the Barbary Coast and somehow relocate her in Colorado. Perhaps set her up in a respectable business of some sort, or at the very least secure her a job a cut above the Bella Union. Yet the fairy tale about his whorehouse empire, and their partnership in the enterprise, was unadulterated poppycock. However good his intentions, he had gulled her with a pipe dream that resulted in her death.

Looking back, he saw now that he'd made a fatal error in judgment. He should have gotten her out of the Bella Union, and once she was safe—only when she was safe—should he have gone off in search of Ned Adair. At the moment, time had seemed imperative, and unwittingly or not, he had elected to jeopardize her rather than jeopardize the mission. In retrospect, it was an unconscionable decision, all the worse because he'd compounded poor judgment with dumb planning. But then, as the old-timers were fond of saying, hindsight was no better than hind tit.

The memory of Nell would never leave him. Nor would he ever wholly absolve himself of her death. With time, he might learn to live with it. One day, perhaps, he might even find justification for the act. Her death, in the larger sense, had brought about the downfall of Frisco's underworld leaders. But that, too, was more excuse than vindication, and in no way would it mitigate what he'd done. The thought of Nell Kimball would remain a burden, and one he deserved. By all rights, she belonged with him now, on her way to Colorado. He wouldn't forget why he stood alone . . . and curiously lonely.

"Hullo, Starbuck."

Knuckles Jackson halted beside him at the railing. Starbuck was instantly alert. A sudden chill settled over him, and it left a residue of uneasiness. His muscles tensed, every nerve stretched tight, yet his expression revealed nothing. He took a drag on his cigarette and tossed it over the side. Then he fixed Jackson with a stony stare.

"Let me guess," he said evenly. "You've got business in Oakland, and you just happened to board the same ferry."

"Not exactly." Jackson's mouth zigzagged in a gash-like smile. "I've got business, but not in Oakland. It's with you."

"I'm listening."

Jackson returned his gaze steadily. "Yesterday, when you had that little talk with Mr. Buckley, he was tryin' to be reasonable about things. He wanted me to make sure you got the message."

"What message was that?"

"He don't want you to show up for the trial."

Starbuck's eyes narrowed. "Guess I had wax in my ears yesterday. You're saying that without me, there's no one left but O'Brien. So you somehow manage to kill him, and when I fail to testify, there goes the prosecution's case. All charges dismissed and Buckley walks away with a clean bill of health."

Jackson gave him a wide, peg-toothed grin. "You're

pretty swift. I wasn't too sure m'self, but the boss said you'd see the light. He figured a word to the wise and you wouldn't come anywhere near that trial."

"And if I do?"

"Too bad."

"Too bad if I show up?"

"No." Jackson touched the brim of his hat. "Too bad you asked the wrong question."

Out of the corner of his eye, Starbuck caught a glint of metal on the upper deck. In that split-second, he realized Jackson had a confederate. The signal, touching his hat, was prearranged. A signal to end it there.

All in a motion, Starbuck pulled the Colt and dropped to one knee. A slug thunked into the wooden railing, followed an instant later by a loud report. He saw a man on the upper deck, squinting at him down the barrel of a revolver. Thumbing the hammer, he extended the Colt to arm's length and let go two rapid shots. The man stiffened, and a pair of bright red dots, centered chest high, appeared on his coat front. He stumbled, arms flapping like a scarecrow, and his legs suddenly collapsed beneath him. The gun went skittering from his hand and he keeled over backward, spread-eagled on the deck.

Starbuck twisted around. The hammer was cocked and his finger tightened on the trigger, then he stopped. Knuckles Jackson stood frozen at the rail, his hands empty and very prudently held in plain sight. His look was one of disbelief, and outright terror. The look of a vicious dog suddenly cornered by a boar grizzly.

Climbing to his feet, Starbuck's expression turned immobile and dark. His eyes flashed with a cold glitter as he took a step closer. A grim line of rage, naked and revealed, tugged at his mouth.

"You sorry sonovabitch! I ought to kill you."

"Nothin' personal," Jackson croaked. "I was just followin' orders."

"Then here's an order for you. Buckley's so keen on messages, I want you to carry one back to him."

Jackson swallowed hard. "Yeah?"

"Tell him for me that I'll see him at the trial."

"I sure will, them very words."

"One more thing," Starbuck said softly. "Tell him if anything happens to Denny O'Brien, I will personally stop his clock, tick-tock and all. You got it?"

"I got it."

"Then start swimming."

"Swimming?" Jackson's face went ashen. "What d'you mean?"

"You heard me." Starbuck commanded. "Hit the water and make like a duck."

"Jezzus Christ!" Jackson bawled. "You ain't serious! I'd drown before I got halfway to shore."

"I'm dead serious." Starbuck wiggled the Colt with a menacing gesture. "You can haul ass over the side or die where you're standing. Only make up your mind *muy* goddamn *pronto!* I'm through talking."

Jackson opted for the water. He gingerly climbed over the railing and hung there a moment, staring down with a look of queasy horror. Then he leaped, his hat drifting lazily in the air, and hit the ferry's wake with a leaden splash. An instant later he surfaced, spewing water, and bobbed about like a cork in a stormy sea. Arms flailing, he finally got himself oriented with the distant shore. He struck off at a slow crawl toward the city by the bay.

Starbuck grinned, watching from the fantail a long while. Then, not at all displeased with the outcome, he shoved the Colt in its holster and strode off in the direc-

tion of the passenger cabin. His step was jaunty, and he
was quietly humming a Frisco ditty to himself.

The next time I saw darlin' Nell
She was gussied up for a spree.
She had a pistol strapped 'round herself
And a banjo draped acrost her knee!